Table of Contents:

CW01513070

Cooped Up

Christine Winston

Cover Designs Copyright © 2015 by Nicole Coroner

Book design and chapter opening illustrations © 2015 by Nicole Coroner

www.twitter.com/nicolecoroner

Acknowledgments

To Isabelle, my beautiful daughter for sharing your Mammy with this book. I love you more than words can say, thank you for your unconditional love x.

To Biddy & John A.K.A *The Parentals* thank you for channelling my wild spirit and penchant for "telling stories" x.

To my little sister Janet for all your angry critiques, your passion for real characters pushed me (because I feared for my life) to create stronger and more passionate characters... I hope.

To Dee for always saying yes! You are the world's greatest aunt. Thank you for being there x.

To my best friend Nicole / proof reader / editor / book cover designer ... I think your title says it all, this book would never be without your advice, encouragement and true friendship. I don't want to get too mushy but I LOVE your face!

#HUMANHAMMER #NAILEDIT #WEDIDIT #20LBSOFDOGFOOD-LATER #24YEARSOFFRIENDSHIP

#YOUDONEHADBEEN

To Bernard, Emma and all my family and friends who supported and helped me.

Thank you all.

X X

Dedication

For Isabelle
I Love You More,
I Love You Most.

Chapter One

The rain fell softy against Cara's face, as she rushed through down town New York. Her shift at the café had run over and she was now late for visiting hours. Like the rain, she decided to pick up her pace; she had twenty minutes to make it across town. She missed visiting hours the day before and knew Mae would be worried. Stopping briefly to prepare, she pulled the belt on her black trench coat and retied the laces on her white sneakers. She would have to run as fast as she could from here. Seeing the Hospital in the distance, she figured she could make it in ten.

Jack hated public relations. He had, in his opinion, just wasted an hours work. Yes, donating to the hospital was a necessary good cause but did he really have to show up to cut ribbons and smile for the cameras? He wanted to donate money for the new children's ward anonymously in honour of his parents, but the press somehow got hold of the information and he was forced to attend today's ceremony. He didn't smile, didn't waste time pretending to laugh at people's jokes or find anything interesting in inane small talk. He hated his picture in the papers.
"David" he called to his PA.
"Yes Mr. Cooper?" David was at his side immediately. Jack hired him two years ago, he'd initially found his personality to be a bit more colourful than he was used to. However, his work was exceptional to say the least, and he came to find his zest for life endearing. David had a flare for fashion choosing to wear dickey bows and

brighter clothing over the typical business suit. Jack had to admit; his style was trendy and suited him perfectly. "I am leaving now. Call the car around" with that Jack turned, said his goodbyes and headed straight for the exit. David trailed behind, firing orders over the phone. Jack hated smiling for the cameras, but not as much as he hated hospitals. The smell had a strange effect on him; it brought a sick feeling to his stomach and the hint of a memory. He felt it rise up within him again as he headed for the exit. He knew deep down the events that fought to creep back up, but he was past that now and would not allow himself to wallow in self-pity.

The sudden battering of rain on his face awoke him from his reverie, washing those thoughts away.

It was raining heavily; New York City was known for being one of the most vibrant and colourful cities in the world, yet today it looked like a scene from an old black and white movie. People ran to find shelter as the wind and rain picked up speed. The thick grey clouds now rolled and clattered as they threatened to open up and strike with lightening. A young man was helping an old woman who struggled to keep her umbrella from blowing away. A father huddled his child beneath his heavy jacket, as they ran towards the hospital.

Jack stood waiting on Lucas, his driver, as the scene unfolded around him. Using his newspaper for shelter, Jack reached for the car door. He wasn't sure what made him look up. Maybe it was the sound of the ambulance siren as it approached or the sudden rumble of thunder or the golden mass of curls heading straight into the ambulance's path. His mind didn't have time to catch up with his feet as they bolted forward.

Cara heard the ambulance siren, but ashamedly she hadn't looked to see where it was coming from. Her face protected by her collars, she raced towards the hospital entrance. The weather had worsened in no time and she was soaked through. In her haste, she barely glanced at the flashing amber lights of the pedestrian crossing as she dashed forwards. In an instant she was lifted from the ground. As if in slow motion, a hard object hit against her chest, propelling her backwards. Crashing onto the cold wet street, she felt pain lance through her right side. Cara now found herself trapped beneath a figure. He was holding her head, his other arm around her back cushioning her from the fall. Her mind fought to figure out what was happening, when an angry male voice erupted from the figure above her.
"What were you thinking?" he spat.
"What the hell were *you* thinking?" she snapped back from beneath him.
"Are you stupid? Running out in front of an ambulance" he condescended, turning angry green eyes on her.

Jack dragged himself and his wounded shoulder off of the slim blonde and up from the ground.
Typical woman! He cursed, *injure yourself trying to help them and* you're *the bad guy!* Reaching down he pulled

her up from the puddle she had landed in. Her soft curves brushed against his leg as she steadied herself.

Cara felt herself lift from the pathway just as quickly as she had landed there. Her body rubbed against his and she felt her fingers tingle at his touch. She felt like a ragdoll, she was about to scold him again for his rough treatment of her when a third man joined them.
"Mr. Cooper, are you okay?" he asked having witnessed the events from the side of a car.
Cara looked at them as they spoke.
"Yes David, we're leaving."
"But Jack.. I mean Mr. Cooper, your shoulder… shouldn't you have it looked at?" with a smirk on his face and pointing behind him he added "there's a hospital right there". Cara giggled a little at David's humour; it was obvious his boss wasn't as amused.
"It's fine; just get me out of here" he said as he turned back to face her.

Jack looked at the woman, she was a wet mess. Her previously bouncy curls were now matted to her face and her clothes dirtied from the fall, he found himself look a little longer than was socially acceptable. She looked like a lost puppy; her pale blue eyes framed in thick black lashes drew him in.
"Look where you're going in future, you could have killed us both with your carelessness" he lambasted her.

"Finish up here David and meet me back at the office in one hour."

He moved towards his car and was already almost out of sight before Cara's mind caught up with what had just happened.

Her side ached from the fall and her feet sloshed inside her white sneakers as she stood, gob smacked at his telling off.

"Don't worry his bark is worse than his bite" Cara turned to the man who had been left behind.

"Hi, I'm David" he stuck out his hand and she took it

"Cara" she replied.

"Who was he?" she asked still shocked by the events.

"Who?"

Cara rolled her eyes "The man who nearly ate me for breakfast."

"I think he just saved your life honey, that ambulance almost squashed you. I thought for sure you were a goner when I looked up. Thank God Jack was quicker than me, I'd have never reached you in time."

"Oh" Cara hadn't realised just how close it had been.

"Not sure I would have risked an expensive designer suit like he did, considering the thanks he got for saving your behind" he nudged her with his elbow as they began walking side by side into the hospital.

"Oh I feel awful now, I got a fright I thought he was attacking me" Cara stopped inside the door and put her face in both her hands. She was mortified.

"You have to tell me who he is, I really need to apologise and check he is okay. He looked hurt" she begged feeling genuine concern for him now.

"His name is Jack Cooper."

"Jack Cooper" she repeated "that rings a bell" she looked up for a moment before shrugging her shoulders unable to make a connection.

"Well it should darling, considering he is the wealthiest bachelor in New York City, heck probably the world" he reported proudly.

"Oh, okay he sounds like a really important man so I doubt I'll ever see him again. Can you thank him for me? Please let him know that I'm so grateful."

"Don't you want to do that yourself?"

Cara considered for a moment if she should seek him out and concluded it would be a bad idea. He had practically run from her as if she was diseased, she didn't need to embarrass herself or put him out any further.

"No David, I don't want to impose on his time any further. If you convey my deepest gratitude I think that would be enough."

"Consider it done Cara. How are you feeling?" he asked, swiftly changing the subject.

"A little sore but I'll live. Thanks for your help" she smiled and bid him goodbye before turning to leave.

"Oh before you go" David called from behind her.

"Can I have your full name please? It's for insurance purposes, nothing to worry about."

"Cara Stone."

***

An hour later, Jack was warm, dry and back at his desk. This was where he felt most at ease, he loved his work. He had used his inheritance wisely when he turned twenty one, putting himself through college and starting his own business. He felt a void after his parents passed away and work seemed to be the only thing that filled it. He built his business up from the ground and now it was a successful multimillion dollar organisation. Leaning back in his chair he turned to look out over New York City, the rain had eased off and the sun was beginning to break through the grey clouds, in the distance a rainbow began to form over the Empire State building. His heart belonged to New York, but when city life got too much, he loved nothing more than to escape to his quite country retreat in Hudson Valley.

His grandfather lived there all his life before he passed away, and despite the fact that it was too big for Jack alone, he couldn't part with it. There was a certain magic about the old property that charmed him. He turned from the view as David entered the office. He was, as always, smiling. Despite having being rained on less than an hour ago; he, like Jack, had changed and was ready to get back to business.

"Sir, how's the shoulder?" David chirped, as he approached the desk.

Jack tried circling his shoulder again, but stopped half way.

"It's fine." He lied. The last thing he wanted or needed was to have his arm in a sling, he hated to appear weak.

"I think you should have it looked at…" David quickly changed tact when he saw the look on Jack's face.

"However, it is none of my business. These are the reports from the lab today" David handed over the thick white envelope. Reaching for the package, Jack grimaced as he tried to hide his discomfort. When David's hands left the documents, the true weight hit Jack and he winced in pain and dropped them on his desk.

He looked up at David, who stood there, lips pursed and eyebrows raised. He could see the *I told you so* trying to burst from his lips. Jack sent him a warning look, and watched him turn on his heels to leave.

"David?" he called through gritted teeth.

"Mr. Cooper?" He returned with a victorious look in his eye.

"Call my Doctor and have him here in the hour."

"I will get straight on it" he began to pull the door behind him, facing away, hiding his smile.

"Oh and David?..What happened with that woman after I left?" Jack asked, despite wanting to forget her.

David had worked with Jack Cooper for two years, in all that time he'd never asked after anyone. Both shocked and intrigued he took a step back towards his boss

"She was a little banged up…nothing too serious" he shrugged, watching Jack who had his head down reading the reports but his shoulders were tense and David smiled. Maybe Mr. Cooper wasn't as indifferent as he seemed after all. David decided to test the waters. Just a little bit. "She was quite worried about you actually, insisted I send her deepest gratitude. I have her information if you need it?"

Jack looked up grunting "Worried about the famous Jack Cooper, was she?"

David assessed his boss "I believe her concern was genuine, Sir."

Jack returned to his reports, picking them up and turning his chair to face away, effectively dismissing David.

***

A week after her brush with death, Cara was still a bit tender. The weather was picking up but her spirits remained low. She was working every odd job that she could get her hands on but the money she was earning was nowhere near enough to pay for Mae's treatment. The café cut her shifts, and would call her if they had any hours available.

The hospital called her that morning to remind her that she would need to provide proof of income and a payment plan to cover Mae's bills or they would release Mae within the week. Unfortunately, after the café had all but let her go the odd gig and busking wasn't considered a steady income and beyond that it wasn't even enough to cover Mae's stay never mind her medication. Cara was all Mae had, they'd relied on each other over the years but the weight of this responsibility was life and death and Cara was not about to give up on Mae.

Maybe things are starting to brighten up Cara thought to herself as she looked through the window of the fancy hotel she was about to perform in. She hoped this gig would lead to something more permanent. Clutching the strap of her guitar case she stepped forward and into the large marble foyer. The staff buzzed about the place, tending to the rich and famous and Cara wished for just a moment she knew how it felt to never have to worry about money. Mae always said that money didn't bring happiness, but right now she would be the happiest woman alive if she had enough to care for Mae.

Cara approached a tall, elegant blonde lady at the reception desk. She needed to change, set up for the evening and meet with Thomas the manager. Thomas had hired her and Cara hoped she hadn't bitten of more than she could chew by agreeing to play here. It was very upmarket and posh and she was the complete opposite.

"Excuse me" she interrupted politely as the lady tapped away on a keyboard.

"One moment" Cara was silenced as the lady lifted her index finger and continued typing without a second glance at Cara. Cara held her tongue at the rude dismissal; she needed this so the last thing she was going to do was address the finer points of etiquette with the snotty receptionist. Taking a deep breath she tried again. "Excuse me, could you tell me…"Cara stopped mid-sentence realising she was being completely ignored. She looked around for another member of staff to help her, but everyone was busy.

Jack looked at his watch again for the fifth time, he hated incompetence. David was to check on their Texan visitors, ensure everything was in order and meet him back here within ten minutes. He was now six minutes late, which meant that Jack was now late for his business meeting. He'd been sitting in the foyer of the hotel when a familiar blonde woman walked through the door. Jack watched from a distance as the slim woman with long wavy hair crossed the marble floor. She lit up the dull room with her golden hair and colourful clothing. The women who walked past her were elegant and well dressed in the best designer clothes.
He watched her closely as she passed him; her unmistakable blue eyes now identified her as the woman he had helped the week before. Her denim jacket looked strange in the middle of winter coupled with a white vest which barely masked her pierced belly button. Jack couldn't help but find her totally endearing. Her big eyes, full of fear, made him want to ease her discomfort. He watched her walk nervously to the reception desk.

"Excuse me, could you please…" Cara continued, hoping to simply get directions into the main bar.

"Mam, I will be with you shortly" dismissed again, Cara turned away from the useless receptionist intending to find her own way. As she turned she crashed into a hard wall of muscle, a familiar smell filled her senses and she stood back to look up into dark angry eyes that bored into hers.

"I'm so…" She started, when she realised who it was and felt her legs begin to wobble. Strong fingers clenched her upper arm and turned her back towards the receptionist.

"Where is your manager?" he growled at the now startled employee.

"He is close by Mr. Cooper, is everything okay? Can I help you?"

"Yes you can, you can apologise to this lady, who you rudely ignored and give her your full, undivided attention."

"Yes Sir, of course. I apologise Mam I was totally out of line, how may I help you?"

Cara felt the pressure of his fingers relax and his powerful body move away from hers. He simply walked away without another word leaving both her and the not-so-composed receptionist with open mouths. Jack Cooper had come to her aid again.

***

Cara changed into her best dress and heels. She'd had it for years but it was chic and elegant and clung to her curves; it was the perfect little black dress for a gig like this. She was asked by the hotel manager to play here for one hour and if everything went well he would give her more work down the line. She had sung at hundreds of open mic nights, but this was the first big hotel to offer her any work. It was fluke really; she'd been singing in a small, offbeat but trendy cafe downtown when the hotel manager Thomas, wandered in looking for directions. He ended up staying for her set and approached her straight away with an offer of work. She looked out now at her audience, everyone chatted amongst themselves paying no attention to her and she sat on the stool in the corner. The soft music that played from the overhead speakers ended and she began to lightly strum her guitar. Thomas requested that she keep it soft and simple, she was to be invisible. Fading into the background was her specialty, she would simply close her eyes and pretend, like they would, that she wasn't there. She began to sing and forget a little about where she was, and just how lost she felt.

A husky female voice filled the dining room creating a warm and sensual atmosphere. It was an interesting choice for this hotel Jack mused, as he sat and listened to the soft music. He was meeting with the head of a rival pharmaceutical company to discuss a joint venture. As always with these dinner meetings countless hours were initially wasted with talk of golf and other mind-numbing subjects. Jack was not known to be a chatty or sociable guy but he smiled when necessary and even commented when he knew he should. Taking precious time out of his busy schedule to talk about golf was not his idea of fun, but he knew business also needed to have the right amount of a personal touch. He needed ViaxaPharm Labs to come on board with his latest research, in order to get FDA approval for continued work on his project.

"Well now would you look at the legs on that little miss" the deep drawl of his Texan dinner companions interrupted his thoughts.

"Well looky here Coop she's coming this way."

Luis, the CEO of ViaxaPharm labs, nudged him. Lifting his napkin from his lap, Jack looked sideways at the approaching figure.

"Excuse me gentlemen, I'm sorry to interrupt but…"

Cara looked down at Jack Cooper, the man she wanted to thank. His eyes bore into hers as he now looked at her like the receptionist had. Twisting her hands in each other she cleared her throat and continued "It's just that I wanted to thank you for earlier *and* for last week, obviously."

Putting out her hand to shake his, Cara was surprised when he stood from the table, buttoned his navy jacket, excused himself and walked her towards the exit without saying a word.

When they reached the doors, just outside the dining area, she began to speak again "I didn't mean to disturb your evening. I just wanted to thank you."

"I'm in a business meeting" his cold flat tone sliced through her.

"I…I only wanted to thank you" she felt her face redden, he was making her feel ridiculous.

"You interrupted an important business meeting to thank me?"

"YES" Cara shot back, her voice slightly raised. "Why is that so hard to believe?"

"You had the chance to thank me last week and instead you accused me of attacking you" his eyes narrowly assessed her as his now deathly calm voice left her feeling like a fool.

"I'm sorry about last week, and I'm sorry about tonight. I only wanted to thank you. I can see that was a mistake. I'll go now" Cara wanted to run as far away from him as possible, he was intolerable. He helped her, yes, but it didn't justify his rudeness.

"Did you follow me here tonight?" he asked suddenly, the hamster in his mind working overtime.

"You have got to be kidding!?!" Cara was appalled at his conceited paranoia.

"It's a bit of a coincidence don't you think? If you thought dressing up and making a play for me in a crowded restaurant would work, you are sadly mistaken" he smirked now, like the cat that got the cream.

A sudden rage like nothing she had ever felt rushed through her, making her eyes pool with both the feeling of embarrassment and anger.

"How dare you speak to me like that, I only wanted to thank you! You are the last man on earth I would dress up for. You are arrogant and rude and I'd sooner be hit by that ambulance than be seen with you" her tongue lashed, slicing through him. Cara turned to complete it with a dramatic exit when she bumped into Thomas.

"That is quite enough Ms. Stone, you can collect your things and leave immediately" Cara swallowed hard seeing Thomas standing there, his face was as red as Jack Cooper's, both men looking like they wanted to throttle her.

"I'm sorry Thomas, but nobody will treat me as if I am below them not you, not your staff and not this asshole, thank you for the opportunity I will see myself out."

Cara had never felt so empowered in all her life as she waltz out of the hotel, she got two blocks before she realised she hadn't been paid and another block before that sinking feeling of dread consumed her again.

Jack bit his tongue as he watched the smart-mouthed wench walk away. He helped her out earlier and in return she'd interrupted his business meeting and then had the nerve to call *him* an asshole! He should have known better, this is what happened when you inserted yourself in other people's lives. She looked vulnerable at the reception earlier that evening, but she was anything but vulnerable. She'd given him a piece of her mind and spat venom with it. He assumed at one point she'd arranged the little escapade to gain his attention, but Thomas's interference quashed that theory. However, he didn't regret his error, she was a joy to watch in all her feisty splendour. He smiled remembering the sway of her hips as she marched out of the hotel. Taking a sip of his whiskey, he sat back in his seat and relaxed into a subject close to his heart, work. He would revisit the images of the fiery blonde later that night.

Chapter Two

David paced outside Jack's office. He hated the fear that stopped him from breaking the bad news to his boss. Jack Cooper was not a man to take no for an answer, he was a ruthless business man who liked things done his way and done to perfection. Despite his boss being a quiet man, he had found him to be at least fair. This however, was the first time David was going to tell him that he couldn't have what he wanted and he knew there would be hell to pay. Taking a deep breath and hating himself for being so spineless David pushed open the door to Jack's office. The fact was, Jack would have to just get over it.

"Sorry to disturb you Sir, but Alesha Andrews has turned down your offer to play at the retreat next weekend." David let out a small sigh of relief at having said it but watched on as Jack lifted his head from his papers to look at him.

Sitting back in his large black leather chair Jack pursed his lips and looked steadily at his assistant. He had to admire the man's backbone; he liked his staff to be straight with him. He didn't need an assistant afraid to tell him as it was.

"Why?"

"Well, she is getting married on Friday and in her own words 'No amount of money will make me miss my honeymoon.'".

"Okay, that is acceptable I suppose. I want you to send her a wedding gift and then make sure we never hire her again. I'd like you to find me someone else who is available next weekend at such short notice. I want them to be available both evenings but they are to have variety, I don't want the same act two nights running."

Jack watched David take notes, nod and turn to leave.

"David before you go, there was a singer playing a few weeks back at the Stanbridge East Hotel, the night we met with ViaxaPharm, look into that first. She was fantastic and if she's good enough for them, I'm sure she'll be good enough for me."

"Yes Sir" David was already phoning Thomas at the Stanbridge East as he closed the office door.

***

Cara sipped over her second coffee at her local diner. She had decided to go for a walk while Mae rested and found herself unable to return home. It was hard to see Mae so ill, but it was even harder to look her in the eye and continue to reassure her that she would find a solution to their money worries. Sitting here spending a few dollars on a coffee was more than she could afford right now, but she needed to get out of the cold and think things through without looking at prescription bottles or listening to Mae be sick. She'd been out busking, and called all her previous employers trying to find some work but nowhere was hiring. Cara covered her face with both hands; she could feel a headache taking root and was finding it impossible to think anymore. She was about to leave when her phone began to buzz, seeing a number she didn't recognise appear on the screen unnerved her. Her stomach turned every time the phone rang or a letter came in the door, she owed too many people money to keep track anymore. Taking a deep breath and hoping it was good news Cara answered the call

"Hi Cara Stone speaking."

"Cara hi, David Lewis here, I work for Jack Cooper, do you remember me?"

Cara sat up straight, the twisting in her tummy worsened by the sound of his name. Jack Cooper was someone she couldn't forget.

"Of course I remember you, is everything okay?"

"Yeah everything is great, how have you been?"

"I'm good… I'm a little surprised to hear from you."

"Well you wouldn't believe the co-inky-dink we've landed ourselves in, I was talking to Thomas at the Stanbridge hotel…"

"Well if this is to do with what happened between me and Jack, if he lost money or something I'm not being held responsible."

"No its nothing like that, Jack wanted to offer you some work."

"Some work? What kind of work?"

"It's a gig next weekend, it's out of town but it pays very well."

"Is this some sort of joke? Is he feeling sorry for me because he lost me my last job?!"

"What? No! Jack has no idea it's you, he spoke so highly of the singer and it was only when I got in touch with Thomas at the Stanbridge, that I realised it was you."

"Well I doubt he will want to hire me when he finds out it's me."

"Why would you think that? Jack was really taken with you at the hotel."

"Ha! Yeah taken right out the front door."

"What the hell went on with you two that night? I didn't realise all this drama was going on in Jack's life."

"Well basically, I showed up at the hotel…"

"Wait wait wait…" the phone fell silent for a moment "Okay, I'm sitting down, tell me everything."

David sat back in his chair, delighted with life. So, his boss met Cara again since he had first helped her and *now* had him tracking her down to work for him next weekend. He was going to convince Cara to do this gig, there was no way he was going to miss this feisty woman disarm the impenetrable Jack Cooper.
David phoned his friend and colleague Jenny, this was juicy gossip too big to keep to himself but he also needed help to hatch a plan.

***

Eight days later, David walked into Jacks office. He waited until the day before the gig, it was a risky move but in order for his plan to work he had to wait until now. He fully expected a serious backlash for what he was about to do but he had no choice.

Jack was just about to leave when David entered.
"Mr. Cooper delighted I caught you, we have a problem with the act for tomorrow night."
"Fix it" Jack said simply picking up his jacket to leave.
"That's the thing, I can't. I have phoned every agent in the phone book the only acts available this weekend are heavy metal bands or Abba tributes."
"What the hell are you talking about David? You told me last week this was sorted. What happened to the act from the Stanbridge?!"
"Well the thing is Cara Stone now refuses to work for you."
"Who the hell is Cara…" Jack paused, he didn't need to finish, he already knew the answer. *Cara Stone again!* The woman was everywhere he went.
"The act from the Stanbridge, I offered her four thousand dollars but she said she would only accept the job if

you apologised personally….Obviously I dismissed that idea."

"APOLOGISE!?" Jacks voice boomed "What the hell for?!"

"That I can't tell you, but apparently you were…"

"I was *what?!*"

David cleared his throat "An ass" he said trying not to smile.

Jack turned and walked towards his window, he stood for a few minutes assessing the situation. He had a choice to make; heavy metal, Abba or go see this crazy woman and *"apologise."*

David watched as Jack churned this bombshell over in his head. Jack's back was to him, but he could tell by the pull of his broad shoulders and the twitching muscle of his jaw, that he was furious. Tycoons the world over couldn't cause him to lose his poker face and here a petite blonde had him eating out of her hands.

"I could leave her details on your desk Sir."

"I will sort something out and this is the last time I will ever do your job for you, you're done for the evening."

***

Jack stood on the door step of the address in Queens David had left for him. He wasn't sure exactly why he decided to come here but he'd thought about this woman for over two weeks now. He had refused to ask Thomas Brighton the hotel manager any information on her and the same with David. It all made sense now why she was at the hotel that night but he hadn't connected the dots beforehand, refusing to indulge in ridiculous fantasies about a complete stranger. Jack was like any red blooded man, he enjoyed women but would certainly never pursue a hippy with a bad attitude; and yet here he was knocking on her door. He stamped down any twinge of desire that stirred in him, this was strictly business and he always got what he wanted in business.

Cara sat on the floor of Mae's bedroom putting the finishing touches to her newly painted walls. She
had picked up some cream paint half price and was painting over the drab mustard colour that had been there for years. Cara wanted to do something nice to cheer her up, she'd been through so much lately. It would mean sleeping on the couch for a few nights, so Mae could have her room but it was a small price to pay.
Jack was led to a room at the back of the house, the sight before him caused him to stop before entering the room. Leaning against the doorjamb he took a moment to let the image sink in. Cara Stone was more beautiful than he remembered. Her long wavy hair was high and messy on her head, with a red bandana doing a terrible job of protecting her from paint splashes. She sat with her legs crossed, wearing ripped denim shorts and a simple grey t-shirt. She was listening to something and humming

quietly along as she concentrated on getting the edges right.

"Damn it" she grunted and he smiled watching her make a mistake.

Cara reached for a dry cloth to wipe the paint she'd just smudged, when she seen Jack Cooper standing in Mae's bedroom. She watched him for a moment, a cocky grin on his face as he stood with his hands in his trouser pockets looking at her. He was dressed in black, high-lighting his dark hair which was unusually dishevelled. His green eyes, as always, moved up and down her body like lasers, scanning for defects. He was so handsome when he stood silent like this but she knew he wasn't here for pleasantries. She placed her paint brush on the edge of the paint tin and pulled her earphones from her ears.

"What are you doing here? Who let you in? Where is Mae?" She fired at him, caught off guard at his sudden appearance and cringing internally at him finding her a mess, covered in paint.

"What can I do for you Mr. Cooper?" crossing her arms she almost began to tap her foot. This was the man who had come to her rescue twice, but both times instead of feeling grateful, he walked away leaving her riddled with insecurities and doubt. He found it so easy to belittle her with just a look and here he was standing in her home, unannounced and unwelcome and she looked terrible. It was like coming up against a dragon without any armour to protect yourself. She felt naked and vulnerable and it pissed her off.

"It's more what I can do for you I think" Jack smiled, he had planned to apologise to get Cara to work for him this weekend, but now realised he could use her circumstances to his advantage.

"What's wrong with her?" he asked pointing towards the other room.

"What?! You came all the way down here to ask me what's wrong with my aunt?"

"Well, by the looks of it that woman should be in a hospital, so I would like you to explain to me why she's here without proper care and proper equipment?"

"How dare you! That is *none* of your business!"

"It's *exactly* the kind of business I'm in Ms. Stone, and by the looks of things what you're doing could be considered neglect and these paint fumes certainly aren't helping!"

Cara stared in disbelief at his audacious remarks, each one igniting her anger at herself, the situation and *again* Mr. Cooper.

"Are you serious?! How dare you walk into my home unannounced and judge me on something you know *nothing* about. Let me tell you Mr. high-and-mighty, while you're sitting in your ivory tower counting your money, us mere mortals are struggling to pay for the drugs you make to help the people we love.

Mae *was* in hospital but they kicked her out. I need fifty thousand dollars to make this right and guess what?! I don't have it! You might think you're in the business of saving lives but you've only made mine harder, *especially* since you cost me my last job! I'm doing the best that I can."

"No you're not".

Cara stormed towards him, her hand raised to slap him, she was just about to stop herself when he stepped forward grabbing her wrist and pulling her tight against his body.

"Oh no you don't Ms. Stone" he said through gritted teeth "Now I'm offering you four thousand dollars that would go a long way towards medical bills, you don't have to like me and you don't have to talk to me but if you're all she has then you have an obligation to her despite your pride."

Jack knew it was a low blow but she deserved it for making him come here to practically beg.

He watched as two tears escaped her eyes and rolled down her cheeks.

"Let my hand go please, I've calmed down."

Jack stepped away and fixed his rumpled suit, stopping for a second to take in the fresh cream blob on his designer sleeve.

"Six thousand dollars will cover her medication and doctors' visits for the next three months. I will do it for that and not a penny less." Cara jutted out her chin and slammed her hands on her hips, hoping he wouldn't take the cost of a new suit out of her fee.

Jack admired her she looked like a feisty angel with her big blue eyes, red nose and balled fists. She had a determined glare in her eyes that told him she would not back down. Part of him wanted to haggle with her, taunt her a little further, get her close again but next time he would settle her with his mouth. She shook with anger and disdain for him, which only further compounded his fantasy of taking her like this, all steamy and passionate. She looked more attractive to him now than any woman had ever before.

"It's a deal. A car will pick you up 9am sharp tomorrow. I will arrange a nurse to stay with your aunt this weekend, simply due to the short notice. I hope you appreciate that, considering I'm overpaying you for the gig."

"I didn't ask you to come here and I don't need your money Mr. Cooper."

"I disagree with you on both counts, Goodnight Cara."

Cara watched him turn and leave. She couldn't believe what had just happened; she couldn't believe she had a gig paying six thousand dollars, she couldn't believe she would have enough money to keep Mae comfortable for a while but most of all she couldn't believe she found Jack Cooper attractive; intensely so. His harsh words fired her up with a strange mix of anger and desire. A small part of her was excited for the weekend ahead.

***

Mae had been up a few times throughout the night, vomiting and in pain. She was Cara's rock after her Mother's death; she took her in and brought her up as her own. Throughout the years Cara, like most teenagers, pushed and challenged Mae enough to drive anyone crazy but she never turned her back on her. The cancer was blocking the entrance to Mae's stomach, chemotherapy helped to shrink the tumour but without surgery soon she would die. Cara sat at the side of Mae's bed as she slept, the painkillers had finally taken effect, allowing her to sleep. The fear that Cara felt for her was like a cancer in itself, she was terrified that she wouldn't be able to come up with a solution to help. Jack Cooper offered her a short term solution but deep down Cara knew they didn't have three months and she would need to think big. She'd managed to save four thousand dollars, maybe with the extra six thousand; Mae's surgeon would do the operation and allow her to pay the balance over time. She would chain herself to the hospital gates if she needed to. The doorbell rang and as Cara turned to kiss Mae goodbye, a tear fell from her eyes. The guilt at leaving her at a time when she was so ill consumed her, *it's only for two nights* Cara reminded herself as she left Mae to welcome the nurse.

"Hi, I'm Dr. Roberts" Cara stood back to allow the tall, middle aged man into her home. He was wrapped up warm in a large overcoat and was carrying a black leather bag. As he entered a small blonde woman, Cara hadn't noticed, followed behind.

"This is Ann, she will stay here for the next two nights. I will stop by in the morning and evening to check on Mae, we will take the upmost care of her while you're away."

Cara shook both Ann and Dr. Roberts' hands before showing them around and going through all of Mae's medication. As she picked up her bag to leave she felt a sense of relief that Mae could have some proper care for the next few days.

"Thank you so much, I can't explain what it means to know she will be taken care of."

"Not to worry Ms. Stone everything is in order, Ann or myself will contact you if we have any concerns."

Cara took the Doctor's large warm hand in hers and shook goodbye. She could tell he possessed a caring nature, it radiated from him and Cara felt confident leaving Mae in his care.

Chapter Three

After an hour , Cara approached a large gated mansion in the Hudson Valley. The drive had been like soup to her soul, after they left the city the views were magnificent. Cara felt like a child as she grabbed the edge of the car door, pulling herself closer to the window. They drove through a tunnel of orange, yellow and brown leaves falling from the large trees that lined the driveway to an old gothic style country house. On either side of her there were acres of land as far as the eye could see. The house itself was like something from an Austen novel; with pointed arch windows and a large wooden door. Cara stepped out of the car and looked up at the stone house, which looked more like a castle. The grounds around the house were filled with rows of flowers and despite the time of year it looked like a summer garden. It was rich with beautiful pink and yellow Chrysanthe-mums. There were lavender and white trees overhanging the river of colourful flowers.

"This way Mam" Cara turned to see the driver, carrying her luggage towards the main entrance.

"Lucas don't worry about my bags" she hurried after him.

"Not at all Ms. Stone" he winked.

"I told you to call me Cara" she scolded him playfully.

"All part of the service…Cara" he finished as he continued on with her bags.

She couldn't help but smile as she took in a deep breath of clean country air, she loved it here already.

The house was just as grand on the inside, the entrance-way was large with a beautiful staircase; it split half-way and led, on either side, to two different wings of the house. Cara was a simple woman with no airs or graces, usually wealth would not impress her but today she was overwhelmed at Jack Coopers home. The realisation that this was just one of his many luxurious homes, made the polarity of their circumstances even more evident to Cara. Life was unfair, how someone like Mae who was a loving and caring woman could be left to die because of a few thousand dollars was so senseless, and here was a man who was mean and heartless with all this wealth and nothing better to do with it than buy the latest cool car.

"Welcome Ms. Stone, I'm Jenny."

A beautiful young woman approached Cara and shook her hand. Cara instantly admired her style; she was dressed in a peplum black jacket, black pencil skirt with a fabulous aubergine blouse. Her silky long blonde hair hung straight and down her back.

"Nice to meet you. This house is wonderful" Cara turned full circle looking up at the large chandelier as she spoke.

"It is beautiful isn't it?" Jenny agreed also admiring her surroundings.

"Let me show you to your room, Mr. Cooper hasn't arrived yet but I assume you will be taking Ms. Andrews's room."

"Ms. Andrews?" Cara's brow knitted as she wondered who Ms. Andrews was and why she would be taking her room.

"Alesha Andrews, you are here to perform in her place…. Aren't you?" Jenny stopped walking and turned back to make sure she hadn't mixed up her guests.

Cara nearly fainted. "Alesha Andrews!?!.. You mean to tell me that I'm here to replace Alesha Andrews, the famous singer and pianist?".

If Cara felt overwhelmed and out of place before, it was nothing compared to the level of inadequacy that she felt now.

"David tells me that Mr. Cooper was very taken with your music" noticing that the blood drain from Cara's face Jenny laughed "Relax, you will do an amazing job."

Cara was overwhelmed, wondering if the guests expected Alesha Andrews and instead would get her.

She sat on the large four poster bed and ran through her set in her mind. The night before had been spent practicing the music she would use over the two nights. She always loved music as a child, it was a way to escape and express herself, but right now it was like a noose around her neck. She felt an enormous amount of pressure to get it right, not only for herself but for Mae. It hadn't escaped her that Jack Cooper was placing an awful amount of faith in her to pull this off and a little part of her insides fluttered at the thoughts of his dark angry eyes. She doubted if he liked her as a person, but he chose her to do this gig and she would be nothing but professional moving forward. Cara looked around the large luxurious room and felt lonely, she usually relished her own company but now she was so afraid of what might happen to Mae it was scary to realise that she had no one else to turn to for support. She thought back to the night before, she'd never been so angry that she wanted to hit someone, even if they provoked her like Jack had it made her think about how highly strung she'd become lately. Even though she was scared to be away from Mae right now, this house, with its beauty and grandeur felt like a refuge, giving her space to breathe and collect her thoughts. She told Jack that she didn't need or want his money but she knew she needed it to help Mae and she wanted, more than anything, the financial stability to do that.

The real issue was that she didn't want to admit to herself that she needed help. She was doing everything in her power to help Mae, from working double shifts at the café when they became available to busking while Mae slept at night. It was hard to accept that it wasn't enough. Everything that Jack Cooper had said felt like an attack but deep inside she knew it was all true, Mae deserved better. Jack Cooper offended her but he had also supplied her with a great opportunity and top medical care for Mae while she was away. Jack Cooper was an enigma; he was unbearable one minute and rescuing her the next. This gig came at a time when she had nothing, after this weekend she would have six thousand dollars to put towards Mae's care and who knew maybe it would lead to more gigs. She lay back on the bed the tension in her stomach was beginning to ease with the release of some of the anxieties that had been suffocating her.

**

Jack was looking forward to sealing the deal with ViaxaPharm after this weekend. He'd worked hard over the last eight months to carve out a contract which would be beneficial to both companies. Though weekends like these were crucial to his business, and great for staff morale, he never could truly relax in large crowds.
He enjoyed his own company and preferred to keep his personal life private. His business was successful still thrilling and exciting him from the lab experiments right down to spreadsheets and PowerPoint presentations. He surrounded himself with nice homes, cars, and, when the mood struck him, beautiful women. He liked being single and despised the idea of falling in love, that emotion was for the weak. Having seen first-hand what falling in love could do to a person, he would never let anyone destroy him like that. Loving someone meant trusting them completely and he never wanted to carry that burden or put it on someone else.

Jenny met him at the door as he entered, filling him in on the guests and assuring him that everything was in hand. "I have settled Ms. Stone in the same room Alesha Andrews was allocated."

Jack stopped in his tracks.

"Jeri Caldwell is arriving later this evening, it was last minute, can we put her in that room?".

He watched as Jenny dropped her eyes to her manifesto.

"Ok yes, we can do that Sir but we have no other suites available for Ms. Stone."

"Ok."

"Well...We only have a staff room available for her sir" she blushed.

Jack contemplated the situation for a moment; Jeri was great to warm his bed from time to time but there was *no way* she would be spending the weekend in his quarters, it would also mean Cara would be staying further away from him but maybe that was good thing, considering his strange attraction towards her.

"Yes, that's fine for her."

"But Sir she is already settled in."

Jenny looked at Jack shocked at his decision, she'd never been asked to move a performer to the staff quarters before. In all the years they had accommodated guests at any of Jacks homes he'd never put an outsider in the staff quarters. *David is right* she thought *things between Mr. Cooper and Ms. Stone run a little deeper.*

Cara decided to familiarise herself with the house and where she would be playing later that evening. She seen Jack coming through the doors like a tornado, his dark hair wet from the sudden heavy rain outside. He was wearing a long dark coat with a black scarf knotted at his neck. Cara watched him as he approached Jenny, no smile, no warm greeting just straight down to business. It was a pity that such a handsome man, with his dark hazel green eyes, chiselled jaw and olive skin seemed so unapproachable. That didn't mean though, that from a distance she couldn't enjoy the view. He was everything a woman could want in a man; strong, handsome and masculine but for Cara he lacked in the personality department. She wondered if there was another side to Jack Cooper that he kept only for that special woman in his life, or in fact if there was a special woman in his life. Cara followed a sign directing her to the main hall and was now behind Jack and Jenny as they walked. She would have never heard any of their conversation had they not stopped and allowed her time to catch up. Now overhearing their exchange,

she was stunned as Jack once again dismissed her as if she held no value. He was doing her a favour by giving her this gig, she reminded herself and took a deep breath to calm her disappointment before she let them know of her presence.

"That's okay Jenny, I'll gather my things and meet you back here in a bit if you like?". She smiled as sweetly as she could to both of them. There was no way Jack Cooper would know just how small he made her feel, he was on a mission to remind her where she belonged. This time though, she would take the high road and it felt like all her Christmases had come at once when even Jack Cooper had the decency to blush.

Lifting her chin she looked at Jack and smiled.

"Mr. Cooper" she nodded before turning back to her room.

Well I guess that settles the question about a special woman in his life she huffed to herself as she packed her bags to change rooms.

Jack paced his room frustrated; Cara Stone floated about in his home like she owned the place. *She looked ridiculous, all casual and sexy in that grey jumper* he thought to himself remembering her oversized sweater which teasingly revealed a bare shoulder. Her mane of wavy hair plaited to one side *this is a party for some of America's wealthiest people and she's dressed like a that.* He scolded himself for allowing her to be a part of it. She was a stubborn, hard-headed woman who he would now have to go and tell how to dress for the next two nights. He left his room and scolded himself again for the little buzz of excitement he felt at the idea of sparring with her once more. He arrived at the room Jenny had given her in error just as she was leaving.

***

Cara opened the door to find Jack about to knock.

"Come to see me off yourself? No need to check my bags Mr. Cooper I'm common but not a thief."

Damn it, so much for taking the high road she cringed, after the words left her mouth.

Without saying a word Jack walked forward causing her to step back into the room. Closing the door behind him, he turned fierce eyes on her.

"Ms. Stone" he began.

"No need for such formalities Jack, you can call me Cara or do I get a staff number?"

"I think we both know that after this I won't be hiring you again. I find your attitude appalling and ungracious. I also find your professional manner to be lacking, is this what you intend to wear this evening?"

His tone was cold and disconnected and Cara could only laugh at how absurd this whole scenario was.

"Do not laugh at me Ms. Stone" he spat.

Cara looked up at him then, her eyes still filled with laughter.

"But I find you hilarious Mr. Cooper…I mean.. Your Highness, was I supposed to bow?"

Cara felt a gentle tug on her jumper pulling her body towards his.

"I don't know what game you're playing with these outfits, but I advise you to stop."

Cara put her hand over his knotted fist still clutching at her grey sweater.

"Let go of me" she whispered her voice trembling with mixed emotions.

When he released her she continued.

"I'm not playing any games you big ape and of course I don't plan on wearing this tonight."

"Good" he replied, his gaze locked on hers and its intensity burning into her.

"Good" she quipped back.

"Good"

Cara broke eye contact and began to giggle at the silliness of their conversation. She was about to face the consequences of laughing at him again but looked up to find him smiling. She felt her heart pound in her chest and her breath catch as his eyes danced with humour. He was incredibly attractive, and no woman would ever be able to deny this smile.

Cara smiled back as the animosity between them disappeared, only to be replaced with a powerful pull towards him. Her eyes widened as Jack took a step forward closing the distance between them and now looking down on her, his smile remained but his eyes darkened with lust as his head began to drop. She inhaled deeply, raising up slowly on her toes to meet him, when there was a sudden rap on the door. Cara jumped backwards, stepping away from him as Jenny entered the room.

"Sorry to interrupt" she said, clearing her throat and trying to hide a smile.

"Are you ready to go Ms. Stone?"

"Yes.. Yes" Cara stuttered as she grabbed her bag and headed for the door, refusing to look at Jack Cooper again.

Jack returned to his room frustrated for more reasons than one. He should never have tried to kiss Cara, she was here to do a job for him and complicating their relationship would only bring him trouble. He would take a step back and leave her alone for the rest of the weekend, this was an important event and he needed his head in the game.

***

Cara lifted the end of her long emerald green evening gown as she made her way onto the custom built stage inside the large dining room. The room was full of guests who were seated for their meal. She wondered briefly, where all these people had come from. The house was hectic earlier as she moved rooms but it seemed mainly to be staff running about getting things in order. It was so surreal to her that all these people would be staying on this property. She decided to wear her hair down and pulled over one shoulder, her dress was backless with a high-neck and it sparkled slightly as she sat down under the spotlight at a beautiful white piano. She began to play some relaxing soft music by composer

Sean Beeson; she became lost in the music as it floated throughout the room. It still amazed her how with the gentle push of each key such beauty could be created, each hand movement was like putting paint brush to canvas; with her eyes closed the collection of notes and tones became a powerful eruption of colour. Cara could see the music as a dance in her mind, her fingers moved across the keys with such effortless fluidity. This particular piece touched a special part of her; as it intensified and quickened her own body swayed with both the rhythm and the sheer exhilaration the music incited inside of her. The passionate piece reached its crescendo and she found herself thinking of Jack Cooper.

The room fell silent almost as soon as Cara started to play. Jack watched as this small woman caused a room full of business men and women to forget for just a few minutes who they were here to impress. He looked on as her golden hair fell over her face. She stroked the piano keys with such grace and precision. The third piece continued to capture the room but this time her deep husky voice had the guests enthralled. Jack listened to the words carefully, watching her naked back flex, her whole body working to create not only the music but the atmosphere around it. She told a story about fear and loss. Jack looked closely and he could see a gentle flow of tears roll down Cara's cheeks, her face etched with raw emotion as she gave a piece of herself to the room.

The lyrics describe a woman's memory of losing her father as a little girl.

"With guitar in hand you sang me sweet lullabies, it's a pity Daddy there was no time for goodbyes" she sang. He wondered what had happened in Cara's life, she seemed to be all alone except for Mae and he wondered why. Cara was so open and honest, not only in how she dealt with him but also in her music. It amazed him that she could share herself with this room full of strangers, Jack would never show his weaknesses to anyone. She left him speechless earlier that evening, and he smiled now remembering it. Despite his own personal attraction to Cara and her lack of professionalism in person, he had to admit, her performance so far was exceptional.

Over an hour later, Jenny came on stage to let her know that some recorded music would play for thirty minutes to allow her a break. Cara stood to make her way to the bar and was astounded when everyone in the room stood and applauded her. She blushed and smiled with deep gratitude. As she made her way to the bar, guests stopped her to shake her hand and show their appreciation.

Reaching the bar, she smiled at the bar tender and ordered a glass of water.

"A pretty lady like you deserves the best champagne in the house" Cara turned to see a tall man tipping his cowboy hat in her direction.

"As nice as that sounds, if you fill me with Champagne I might end up *dancing* on the piano instead of playing at it."

"I doubt that would be a bad thing" he winked and Cara giggled "I must say, you sure have captured the room with your beautiful playing" he smiled.

"Thank you" she replied shyly.

"I'm Luis, nice to meet you."

"I'm Cara."

She noticed his wedding ring as he took her hand and relaxed a little. The last thing she needed was a cowboy trying to pick her up.

"Do you work for Mr. Cooper?" she asked.

Luis laughed.

"I think you'd have to be crazy to work for that hard ass, but he is a genius that's why I'm considering a joint venture with him."

"I don't really understand what it is he does" Cara shrugged.

"I believe he has his hand in many pies, if ya know what I mean" he winked again "but his Pharmaceutical Company is his main priority, that's where I come in."

"What is it you do?" she asked sipping some water.

"Why don't I tell you over dinner sometime?" Cara almost choked on her water causing her to cough, and in turn had Luis lightly tapping her back.

"MS. STONE" a harsh voice interrupted, Cara's head snapped sideways to see Jack standing there and he looked angry. Again.

"I believe the guests are waiting for you to resume playing" his head looked towards the stage.

Taking the hint she made her getaway "certainly Mr. Cooper" Cara turned placing her glass on the bar .

"Nice to meet you" she nodded to Luis, avoiding eye contact and hell bent on discouraging any further advances. She moved away ignoring Jack and making her way back to the stage.

Jack's eyes followed Cara as she climbed back up on stage, both himself and Luis transfixed as she took her seat back at the piano.

"That is a fine looking woman" Luis whistled.

"Luis, delighted you could make it, pity Sarah was too ill to attend" Jack grinned his eyes giving away nothing of what he really felt about Luis's behaviour. He overheard Luis ask Cara for dinner and witnessed her fumbling about over his attention. He was a smart man, he would never miss a business opportunity because of what other people did in their spare time, but he hated cheaters. He could never understand why men or women who wanted to sleep around would commit to someone else in the first place.

He thought again of how Cara had looked smiling up at Luis, he didn't like it. She was not here to seduce married men and he would tell her exactly how he felt on the matter before she retired for the night.

Cara began her last song for the night. She had seen Jack circulate the room all evening with a particular dark haired lady on his arm. She couldn't see her clearly but she looked like a beautiful woman and wondered why Jack still seemed unhappy. She watched him take her hand and join the other couples on the dance floor. Cara admired his companion's tight red dress, they were such a handsome couple. It disappointed her that Jack had tried to kiss her earlier this evening, even when he had this beautiful woman on his arm. Her eyes moved throughout the rest of the room, and she felt a pang of jealousy. Couples embraced each other, their bodies intertwined and moving together as they allowed the music to guide them. She glanced at Jack again and in that moment their eyes met for a split second and her tummy burst with butterflies. *Uh-oh not good Cara* she really didn't want to have a crush on Jack Cooper.

***

Cara walked the long carpeted corridor back to her room. It'd been a long night and she was exhausted. Her arms ached and she longed to soak in a hot bath. Though she was tired, she was also proud of herself. The crowd seemed pleased and Jack hadn't said anything, which in her opinion, was a good thing.
"CARA!"

Cara nearly jumped out of her skin at the call of her name. She turned to see Luis approaching and looked towards her room; she didn't feel comfortable with him following her.

"I almost missed you" he smiled taking her hand and kissing it.

"Luis I'm just about to go to bed, it was nice to meet you" she pulled her hand gently.

"Would you like me to escort you to your room?" he winked.

"No thank you, you're a married man. Goodnight" she was too tired to beat around the bush. He needed to get the hint and she needed her bed.

"That is true, but why should it stop us having a little fun?"

He was so blatant in his disregard for his wife and Cara found herself stunned.

"Well, it would stop me Luis.. I'm not the kind of girl to go running around with married men. Now, I'm tired and I don't mean to cause you any offence but nothing will ever happen between us and so I'm going to say good-night" with that Cara smiled and turned towards her room and from behind her heard the sound of him pressing the elevator button. She was relieved *hopefully he's got the message.*

***

Cara stepped out of her dress and ran a bath, she may have been sleeping in the staff quarters but she had to admit it was like a hotel room all the same. She was pouring some lavender oil into the water when she heard a knock on the door. Exasperated she pulled a large white fluffy housecoat on as she made her way to the door, preparing to rebuff Luis again.

Jack Cooper was standing in the doorway when she answered it.

"Jack" she said surprised to see him here.

"Sorry to disturb you Cara, but we need to talk can I come in for a minute please?"

Cara clenched her housecoat tighter together as she stepped aside to allow him entry.

"This won't take long" he said his eyes darkening as he took in her state of dress.

"I'm sorry, I wasn't expecting anyone to knock this late I was about to get in the bath" she found herself apologising for how she looked.

"Well I should hope so...that's why I am here actually."

Cara looked quizzically at him "I'm sorry, I don't understand."

"Let's not play games Cara, I seen you earlier flirting with Luis Grayson and I'm here to warn you not to mix business with pleasure."

"Thank you for the warning, I'll take that into consideration" she huffed, folding her arms across her chest.

"Don't get funny Cara, he is an important associate of mine."

Cara noticed he seemed to be getting frustrated "I'm here to do a job, I'm not here to flirt. Yes I was flattered but I noticed his wedding ring Jack. I'm not that kind of girl, but if he was single maybe I would have went on a date with him, despite your opinion on it" she kept her voice even and calm.

"If you're looking for a wealthy man, shop elsewhere" he spat at her.

"That is twice you have implied that I am some sort of gold digger, if I recall correctly *he* came looking for *me.* I am not interested in *you* or your friends" she pulled the door open.

"Please leave" her teeth chattered together, her whole body shook. It wasn't right that he treated her with such disdain. She was about to throw him out when she noticed steam coming out from under the bathroom door.

"Oh crap" she yelped as she rushed to the bathroom. The bath was overflowing, Cara stood at the door frozen for just a moment as she took in the mess. Jack pulled her to one side and cursed as he rushed to turn off the taps. He took off his black suit jacket and reached in to pull out the stopper. Cara kicked off her slippers and rushed to get towels to mop up the wet floor. She let out a yelp as she felt her foot slip forward causing her to land on her butt. The warm water seeped through her house coat, soaking up some of the water. Turning over she used the towels to soak up as much water as she could. She looked up expecting to see Jack run for more staff only to find him reaching for towels and kneeling in the wet to help her.

Jack watched as Cara's face filled with amusement at her own clumsiness, her long blonde hair touching the wet floor as her head fell back in laughter. He was about to call the staff to help but instead reached for towels and joined her on the floor. He stared as she wiped the floors vigorously unaware that her housecoat had fallen open slightly showing just a hint of her full breasts.

They both worked side by side until all of the heavy water was off the floor.
"I'm sorry, I forgot about the bath. I will pay to have all these towels replaced" she offered blowing hair out of her eyes. Jack couldn't help but smile at how cute she looked.

Jack smiled at her, and her heart sank, it was like a scene from a romantic movie. He was kneeling on her bathroom floor, his white shirt and pants almost soaked through. His normally perfect hair flopped over his eyes and his large white smile caused her stomach to flip. She watched as he pinched the wet shirt and pulled it gently from his chest. They both sat there staring at each other, both smiling for just a heartbeat too long causing the air to grow thick. Cara broke eye contact first and began flustering.

"I'll make sure to sort the towels" she swallowed hard.

"I can afford to lose a few towels, don't worry about it" he stood up and reached out his hand to help her to her feet.

"You'll need to get out of those wet clothes before you get sick" she said, trying to break the tension but only making it worse as her eyes travelled down his hard body.

"Is that a proposition Ms. Stone?" his eyes darkened as he watched her bite her lip.

"No, I, I didn't mean that to sound um…" she stuttered, her eyes wide with innocence.

"Calm down Cara I was joking" Jack reached for his jacket to leave "I better go" he turned towards the door.

"Jack" Cara called to him before he left "I, umm… thanks again."

"I must say it seems calamity follows you… Try not to get into any more trouble Miss" he shot her a slanted grin and drew the door closed after him. She cursed herself after he'd gone, she looked like a bumbling idiot.

Jack walked back to his room. Earlier he'd contemplated the idea of spending the night with Jeri, but he found himself uninterested in what she had to offer. He was wet, tired and on dangerous ground where Cara Stone was concerned. He'd wanted to laugh when Cara slipped on her butt, but even worse he wanted to help her out of her soaked robe and not because he was a nice guy. He would fantasise for the rest of the night about what secrets lay hidden beneath that fluffy housecoat. Since she had come crashing into his life a few weeks ago, she seemed to be everywhere he turned. He found himself drawn to her, if he was honest with himself all his frustrations at her, all his demands and ridicule was his way to fight the attraction he felt towards her. He was trying to push her out of his life and all that did was make him realise he wanted her, not to marry or love her but in his bed to satisfy him until he, like always, grew bored. There was a spark between them, she was everything he didn't like, she dressed like a gypsy one day and then tonight like a goddess. Her hair was always wild and messy, usually flowing down her back or in tangles high on top of her head. Her big blue eyes were defiant and feisty one minute then sad or laughing the next. She had a smart mouth that could tear him to shreds in an instant or fill a ballroom with its husky intoxicating sound. Cara Stone was not like any woman he had ever bedded before and he suddenly figured out why he was so attracted to her now. She was a challenge, and women had never challenged him before, they always threw themselves at his feet. Jack stripped himself of his wet clothes and stepped into a hot shower, he would need to figure out a way to keep Cara Stone around for a little bit longer.

***

The following evening Cara used a mixture of her guitar, piano and singing to entertain the guests. It had been a success and Cara was so relieved to be getting back home to Mae the following day. She had phoned earlier that morning and spoke with Ann, who informed her that Mae was still uncomfortable despite treatment. The doctor decided that if she didn't improve by morning she would need to be moved to a hospital. Cara hoped this wouldn't be necessary; they needed to keep what little money they had for Mae's medication and towards her operation. If they took her to the hospital they would only make her comfortable and send her home after a few days with little or no improvement and a big bill. Cara stayed for one drink before she decided to go to bed, it was so strange to be in a room full of people and yet be totally alone. Cara looked around the room; she found herself looking for Jack throughout the night. He hadn't said anything to her at all since last night and he barely made eye contact with her this evening. She spotted him just outside on the terrace, he was speaking on the phone and just as her eyes reached him, he looked up and stared straight at her. The look he gave her was serious, his eyes searching hers. He put his phone into his pocket and turned back to his guests. Cara decided interrupting him regarding her payment was a bad idea, he was busy enjoying his night she would catch up with him the next day.

Taking one last sip of the champagne she headed for bed. Walking towards the exit she felt her arm being grasped and Jack leading her out the door. When they walked outside Cara stepped away.

"I was leaving already, there was no need to drag me out."

Jack looked at her confused "what?"

"I said I was already leaving, I didn't plan on having another drink."

"I don't care if you have ten drinks Cara, we need to talk."

"I was hoping to talk actually about my payment, I wondered if..."

Jack took her arm again and walked her further towards her room.

"I will take care of that, but right now you need to leave...."

"Tonight? Why? What are you talking about?"

"I want you to stay calm Cara, it's your aunt. Dr. Roberts just called she is currently being transported to hospital. Her condition has deteriorated and she's asking for you."

"Oh my God."

"'Cara, she is in good hands, Lucas is free to drive you back to the city, I would myself but I've had a few drinks."

Cara turned and ran towards her room; she began to pull all her belongings into her overnight bag.

Jack followed her "are you ok?" he asked.

Cara stopped what she was doing and nodded, she couldn't speak, tears rolled down her face and she quickly wiped them away. When she was all packed he led her towards his car, he took her bags and placed them in the boot as she climbed into the back seat.

"Thank you" Cara smiled weakly as he closed the door.

Chapter

Four

When she finally reached the hospital it was 3a.m. Cara rushed to reception to try to get some information. A male nurse led her into a room to wait for a doctor to come free. Cara sat there alone for almost two hours; she was too worried to sleep and too tired to cry. The male nurse had told her that Dr. Roberts and her nurse Ann had gone home as there was nothing else they could do. She was just about to go get a coffee when a tall, slim blonde Doctor came into the room.

"Are you Cara?" she smiled, putting Cara a little at ease.

"Yes, is Mae ok?" she couldn't wait any longer she needed to know how Mae was doing.

"She is in recovery, we removed the tumour that was blocking the entrance to her stomach but she may still need one maybe two doses of chemotherapy to kill any other cancer cells that may develop."

Cara felt her knees go weak "she had the operation?" An overwhelming sense of relief washed over her, and she burst into tears. Mae was going to be okay.

"Yes, didn't anyone tell you she was in theatre?"

"No" She sniffed "but how? Her insurance is up, she can't afford it" Cara froze realising the bills that would ensue.

The Doctor began reading through Mae's chart "It looks like a Mr. Cooper has funded the cost of the operation and any further treatment necessary" flicking the pages back in place the doctor looked at Cara again "do you know him?"

"Yes, I do" Cara sat down on the seats provided as she absorbed everything that she was told. Mae had her operation, so far it was a success and Jack Cooper once again was their hero. Her hero.

"Can I see her, doctor?"

"Not tonight, she needs plenty of rest. Come back tomorrow evening and we will arrange for you to see her."

Cara stood and walked over to the beautiful Doctor and shook her hand.

"Thank you doctor, I can't tell you enough what this means."

***

Cara sat in the lobby of Cooper Pharmaceuticals for the third day in a row. Mae was recovering well and Cara needed to thank Jack and attempt to pay him back. It was almost two weeks since Mae's operation and Cara was trying everything to get in touch with him. This was her last resort but she was determined. Jack had sent a cheque for six thousand dollars a few days after Mae's operation and Cara needed to return it, and her savings, to pay her debt. She visited Mae that morning and was now free to sit here all day if she needed to.

The stress of Mae's illness had really begun to take its toll, however things were finally beginning to look up after the operation; the relief was like a new lease of life. Jack Cooper saved Mae's life and Cara was determined to repay him anyway she could. Cara sat reading a book for most of the afternoon, she was just about to pack it in for the day when she seen him.

It was the sound of the wind bursting through the doors as he entered, that made her look up. He moved across the marble floors with a determined look on his chiselled face. His strong jaw shadowed with dark stubble, only improved his sex appeal. The cut of his dark navy suit pulled tight against his strong legs with each stride.

He looked so handsome, and Cara felt her stomach flip at the mere sight of him. She stood up from her seat, clenching her book in both hands and watched him speed past without so much as a sideways glance. Cara's mind screamed at her to call him, to run after him but her body was unable to catch up in time. He was gone in the blink of an eye. She was just about to give up hope when David followed through the doors with just as much speed, but thankfully she'd composed herself enough to act quickly.

"David" she called as he dashed to catch up with his boss. His head spun in her direction and she was instantly put at ease when his face warmed and smiled

"Cara" he replied, seeming pleased to see her again "What has you here?".

"David I need to see Jack" she turned on her puppy dog eyes.

"Why didn't you arrange an appointment at the desk?"

"I tried, but he is booked up for the next three weeks and I really need to see him sooner, please, it will be five minutes, I promise" she pleaded. David began laughing at her attempt to win him over with a pout.

"Come with me, he'll kill me but how can I refuse you darling."

"Oh David, I don't want to get you into trouble just show me where to go and I'll say I snuck in" Cara giggled as they entered the lift. David turned to her with a mischievous look in his eye.

"You know what, I think that's a great idea, you're better to catch him off guard."

Cara didn't know why but she felt like David was enjoying messing with his boss, which surprised her, as Jack seemed like a hard ass.

"Aren't you worried he'll find out?"

"I'll bring you to the office, and before I get to announce you, I will get called away urgently. How you decide to go on after that is your own business" he winked.

David did exactly as he said and Cara found herself at large double doors. Knowing Jack was behind them sent her stomach into overdrive as fear and desire consumed her. It was now or never, maybe it would all go horribly wrong but she couldn't sleep knowing what Jack had done, she needed to repay him. Knocking softly she waited for his call to enter. When it didn't arrive she decided to just look inside and make sure he was there.

Jack heard the gentle knock on his door and ignored it. David never knocked. Whoever it was, they could wait, he was too busy to deal with interruptions right now. He had been in Texas the past week and needed to finalise the contracts for the upcoming merger. He was leafing through the documents when he seen movement in the corner of his eye, looking up he noticed for the first time that Cara Stone was in his office. She walked over to him without a word and was standing nervously in front of his desk. His heart beat harder in his chest as he watched her lick her bottom lip, tugging it gently with her teeth. She was, as always, stunning. Her hair was swept up on one side, the rest falling in waves down her blue blouse, the top two buttons open. His pulse quickened as her soft breasts rose and fell with her laboured breath. She was nervous and it thrilled him that he affected her. Her blouse was tucked into dark indigo jeans that his fevered mind imagined peeling away from her smooth skin. She was a temptation too big for any red blooded man to withstand. She looked at him with an emotion he couldn't recognise and he found himself speechless for just a moment.

"How did you get in here?" sounding harsher than he wanted to, he noticed her visibly flinch at his words.

"I'm sorry to disturb you at work, I really needed to see you, can we talk please?"

Jack hated that he wanted nothing more than to kiss her right now. She showed up at his office unannounced in yet another tempting outfit and all he wanted to do was pin her to his desk and have his way with her. He didn't like it.

"I have a lot of work to get through" he looked at his watch, anything to drag his eyes from hers.

Cara watched him check the time and felt like an inconvenience.
"I know, I won't take long" she twisted the handle of her guitar case.
"Go ahead" he nodded and returned to looking over his papers.
"I came here to give you this" Cara reached into her purse and pulled out an envelope and placed it on his desk.
"That's four thousand dollars in cash plus the cheque you sent. I plan to pay you back every dime for Mae's operation, I can't thank you enough…"
"There's no need, I did it because I wanted to. If I wanted the money you would have heard from me" Jack interrupted.
"I can't accept that, please take this and I'll pay the rest back each month over time… I mean, if that's ok with you?"
Jack sat back in his large leather chair and assessed the situation, he was attracted to this woman who intrigued and excited him. He thought about her more than once when he was alone and now she was here, in his office looking to repay him for helping her aunt. He was clever enough to see an opportunity when it presented itself.
"My housekeeper is away from next week for one month. I'm stuck without her, so here is what I propose;

you cover her for the month, cooking, cleaning etc. it's a live in position and I expect you to cater to all my needs for that month and you can consider the debt paid. Talk to David on the way out he'll make all the arrangements."

Cara looked at him shocked, he hadn't asked her to take the position, and he didn't even make it an option. Cara wanted to throw something at his head. This man was so rude and obnoxious, but she felt indebted to him. She would do everything he asked of her and knowing she had worked off her debt would allow her to sleep easier at night. Cara waited a little bit longer, realising he was obviously finished with her she readied herself to leave when he looked up.

"Is that all?" he began to dismiss her, his eyes void of any emotion.

She pressed her lips together and nodded firmly. *Damn it* she cursed herself, wishing she'd left a second earlier, hating the fact that he got the chance to oust her once again.

She left his office, leaving the envelope on his desk and went in search of David.

David was pacing outside the office when Cara walked out. He'd tried to listen in a little but the oak doors were practically sound proof.

"Hey, so glad you're here" she sighed relieved to see him "Jack wants me to cover his housekeepers holidays next week, said you would arrange everything?"

"What? That's odd Jack never mentioned that before" he smiled "lucky Julie" he pursed his lips to contain his joy at the situation.

"I'm sure it slipped his mind" Cara shrugged.

"Yes, he sure does seem to be forgetting himself lately" David smirked. "Don't you worry about a thing, I'll call you when I speak with Julie."

"Great!" Cara rolled her eyes feigning excitement "Can't wait to dust his shelves."

That's not the only thing you'll be dusting David thought; Jack Cooper's personal life was all but non-existent since Cara had arrived on the scene. The urge to play havoc with Jack's resistance ate at him and he folded, his naughty side winning once again.

"There is a uniform, what size are you?"

"Seriously? I'm a 6, looks like I can say goodbye to colour for the next month" she moaned.

"Don't worry about a thing, Lucas will pick you up next week and I'll have Julie run through everything with you before she leaves, and your uniform will be there when you arrive" closing his notebook he leaned in, kissed her cheek and went on his way.

***

Jack's condominium was overlooking the East River, on the Upper East Side of Manhattan. The apartment building was floor to ceiling glass on all sides. Cara stepped out of the car and walked into the lobby where she met Julie and was formally introduced to the concierge. Cara watched as Julie typed a code into a keypad adjacent to the elevator.

"This lift will bring us directly into the apartment" Julie explained as the steel doors slid open and they stepped inside "everyone has their own access code, you can use mine".

The doors opened revealing a large open plan living area. Floor to ceiling windows wrapped around the space and a curved staircase to the left separated the kitchen and led to an upstairs landing.

"This is the main living area, Mr. Cooper rarely sits in here so you are really only required to polish and maintain it most of the time" Julie chimed as she passed the living area towards the staircase. Rounding the curve of the staircase Cara stepped from the plush carpet onto the white tiles of the kitchen floor. Julie went over everything Jack liked to eat and was adamant that she followed the strict menu she had prepared. Cara cringed at how dedicated Julie was to her job and doubted she would be able to maintain the same standard. Walking through the rest of the apartment felt like a grand tour of The White House, nothing was out of place, not even Jack's socks, which Julie actually pressed. Peeking into his underwear drawer sent a ripple of desire down her spine, even if it was Julie who opened it up. Jack Cooper was a neat freak and that was going to cause a few hiccups along the way.

***

It was a long day and Julie had skipped out leaving her to cook Jack's dinner. Cara looked at the ingredients before her, *chicken and vegetables couldn't be too hard to cook, could it?*
She considered ordering in some take out and pretending the oven didn't work but then she'd have to break the oven.
Jack arrived home to a mouth-watering aroma wafting throughout his condo. Tired after a long day he was starved. The smell pulled him towards the kitchen. Looking at his watch, he wondered why Julie had stayed on to cook his dinner before leaving. His stomach dropped at the idea that maybe Cara hadn't showed up. He turned the corner into the kitchen and almost hit the floor at the sight before him. Cara was bending over into the oven in a French maid's uniform.
"Is this some sort of joke?" he growled.

Cara stuck the thermometer into the chicken to make sure it was cooked all the way through. She was just taking it from the oven when the angry tones of Jack's voice made her jump, causing her to bang her head and drop the dinner all over the floor.

"Ouch" she yelped as the hot dish burned her hand and crashed to the floor.

"What the hell Jack?! I worked hard all day on that!"

"Why are you wearing that ridiculous outfit Cara? I don't find it funny."

"You made me hurt myself and ruin the dinner because you don't like your own staff uniform?"

Turning on the tap Cara ran cold water over her hand.

"I don't have a uniform, you silly woman where would you get an idea like that?" Jack bent to remove the broken dish and food from the floor.

"No leave it, that's *my* job" Cara knelt down to help him.

"I'll do it, fix your hand."

"No" Cara almost yelled as she tried to pry the dustpan and brush from his hands.

"Please Jack, this is my job, I want to do it right, please" Jack's hand relaxed on the dustpan letting it go, he stood and took her hand, bringing her back to the sink.

His callous thumb gently rubbed her hand under the cold water. Cara stood unable to breathe as the air thickened between them again. He looked up from her hand and their eyes met; their mutual desire evident to them both.

"Keep your hand under the water for ten minutes Cara. Don't worry about dinner, I'm not hungry." Jack cleared his throat as he stood back from the sink and turned to leave.

"Great, guess I'll starve for the night too" she said under her breath.

Cara decided to go get some Chinese, and returned to find Jack still in his study. He had been there since ruining dinner and she was nervous about disturbing him. It was her first night and already it was a disaster, he was being a stubborn mule, denying he was hungry. Jack's unpredictable moods were intimidating and it made her stay here feel awkward. Cara hadn't thought to ask if she should knock before disturbing him, or was it part of her job to be invisible? She hated the politics of it all. She knocked and walked in without waiting for an answer, deciding that when in doubt being herself was the safest bet.

Jack was sitting on a sofa beside a large open fire that lit up his study with a warm glow. His bare feet were crossed and resting on a foot stool in front of the fire. His hair was messed as though he had run his hands through it a few times. He was reading from papers held in his right hand whilst stroking his jaw with the other. As Cara approached she noticed how deep in thought he looked and felt her stomach clench. He was so sexy and she hated that she felt that way about him. Jack was usually as straight as a pin and now looking so pensive and dishevelled he seemed casual and open, almost like a normal person. In here she didn't feel out of place in her leggings and another of her favourite jumpers. She assumed he wouldn't mind that she had taken off that ridiculous uniform, from his reaction earlier she suspected David was playing games, she smiled now thinking about it as she moved closer to Jack.

"Sorry to disturb you Jack, but I picked up some take out if you're hungry?"

Jack looked up from his papers and his body instantly hardened at the sight before him. Cara was standing beside the fire, her hands knotted as she stood nervously before him. She was wearing a knitted blue jumper that made her blue eyes sparkle, with her long golden hair falling in waves down her chest. She wore no makeup, and her creamy skin was glowing from the heat of the fire. He preferred her like this, in her own clothes, naturally beautiful and innocent.

He wasn't sure how he was going to seduce her, she wasn't like other women. He hadn't taken the time to think this through. She looked amazing and she was here, under his roof, in his kitchen, his study, sleeping down the hall and he had no game plan. He figured Cara Stone would be a tough nut to crack, but he was up to the challenge. All he needed to do was give her some attention, that's what women wanted more than flowers and chocolates. He learned that from his previous lovers and it was the reason why eventually he left them. Sooner or later they wanted more of him than he was willing to give them.

"Sounds great, what are we having?" he looked up turning his famous Cooper smile on her.

He watched her blush deepen as she licked her lips. Her eyes moving to his smiling mouth.

"Chinese, will I bring it into you?" she answered quickly.

"Yes, we can eat in here if that's ok with you?" he couldn't help the second smile that crossed his face as she tried to compose herself.

"Uh-huh sure, I'll go grab it" she turned and Jack's eyes devoured her sumptuous curves as they sashayed from room. He fixed himself before laying the scene for his seduction.

Cara wasn't sure why she found Jack's smile so dazzling, but every time he turned it on her she was completely disarmed and ended up floundering about like an idiot. She took a few minutes in the kitchen to collect herself before returning to his study. She looked down on the tray she was carrying and hoped she had made the right choices. She wasn't sure what to order so she decided to get a bit of everything; ordering stir fried beef, sweet and sour pork, rice, chicken curry and not forgetting her own favourite, fried noodles.

In Mae's they just ate straight out of the box with forks, but she brought plates and chopsticks with her just in case her way was too common for King Cooper. When Cara returned to the study Jack had pulled a coffee table over to the sofa. He moved to one side of the small leather couch, making room for her. Cara was contemplating whether or not to eat straight from the box when Jack reached forward, grabbed a fork and began to eat from the box. She was so relieved.

"Why are you giggling? Are you a chopstick person? I'm a fork man." Jack turned his head, cocked an eyebrow and looked at her from under his lashes with a slanted grin "Does that make you think less of me?"

Cara grabbed the box of noodles and leaned back against the sofa, intent on breaking his smouldering gaze. Talking into her noodles she replied.

"I'm just surprised to see you so... so normal."

"It doesn't taste the same if you don't eat it out of the box" he smiled leaning closer to take some of her noodles. Cara felt her breath catch at his nearness and his intoxicating smell. He had a cheeky look in his eyes and Cara found herself wondering if he was flirting with her. The absurdity of that thought brought her crashing back down to reality, Jack Cooper might eat from a Chinese box but she figured his taste would be a little more discerning when it came to his women. They both ate in companionable silence, it felt nice to just ease back into the comfy sofa with the blaze from the fire lighting the room in an orange glow.

"How is Mae?" he asked, standing up to turn on some music and pour some wine.

"She's doing great, and she looks great...she should be able to get out of hospital next week, which is great" she beamed nervously.

"That's great!" Jack smirked and Cara chuckled at his playful jibe.

"Dr Roberts and Ann are doing a brilliant job, he called me today to tell me she is doing well."

Cara bit down on her bottom lip, she knew she was here to repay her debt to Jack but he kept helping and her debt kept growing.

"I know what you're thinking, stop. It's already done she needs full time care" his tone was firm.

"But, I can't keep letting you pay for Mae's care; it's crazy, why are you being so kind?"

"I'm not kind Cara, I need you here this month, I needed you to entertain my guest a few weeks ago, it is and was for selfish reasons both times" his eyes darkened and the shutters came down.

"That's the most ridiculous thing I've ever heard, why would anyone pay all that money for no reason? You don't fool me" Cara stood up smiling to clear up the discarded boxes.

Jack walked over to place his wine on the mantelpiece "Oh really? Well why did I do it Cara? Did I do it for you?"

"No" she snapped pulling her shoulders back and staring him straight in the eyes.

"You have made it clear how you see me, and that's fine. I think you did it, because behind all the bravado you're a nice guy" shrugging her shoulders she continued "but then again maybe you're just bored."

Cara bent to continue clearing up. She was about to lift the tray from the table when she felt her arm being tugged and her body crash against Jack's. She looked up into fierce eyes and knew she had angered him. *To hell with it* she wouldn't spend the next month tip toeing around Jack Cooper; afraid to say the wrong thing, dress the wrong way or breathe the wrong air. She stuck her chin up in defiance.

"I'm bored am I? Well why don't I entertain myself?" Without warning; Jacks hand came around her neck, pulling her to his mouth as his lips came crashing down hard against hers. She gasped at his force allowing his tongue entry as it dipped and caressed hers passionately. His other hand came around her waist as he pulled her body up against his own, holding her upright. Her knees weakened as his fingers tangled in her hair and a growl escaped his lips. Cara allowed herself be swept away for a moment as the intensity of their kiss consumed her mind, body and soul. He moved one hand to her ass, squeezing it gently and causing her to snap out of the moment long enough to realise what she was doing. Suddenly aware she pushed at his chest, her head twisting to free herself from this passionate embrace. The burning desire he stirred within her was all consuming, she was threading in dark territory.

Breathless she pleaded "stop" her body trembled with both pleasure and anger. She wasn't sure how to react, so she gave him a piece of her mind.

"You had no right!"

"You wanted it just as much as I did."

Cara was amazed at how composed he was before she realised it was a game to him.

"I would rather spend the night vomiting than do that again, in fact the thoughts of it is making me sick right now" she quipped.

"I don't think so." he returned to get his wine, putting some distance between them. Cara wanted to slap his smug face but she wouldn't allow him to turn her into a raving lunatic. She decided that she would play him at his own game and began laughing, not just a giggle but a deep belly laugh and looked up at him with a sense of victory, as she noticed his face turn red.

"Tell yourself whatever you want, I'm going to bed" she turned to make a triumphant exit.

"Aren't you forgetting something?" he growled.

"Nope was just about to get them."

Cara grabbed the tray, finished her chores for the night and went straight to bed more confused about Jack Cooper than ever.

After Cara left, Jack went back to his papers, but it was impossible to concentrate. He could hear her banging away in the kitchen for a few minutes and it lightened his mood to think that she really didn't care about angering him. She was a force to be reckoned with when she got annoyed but he liked her gutsy nature. He'd been a bastard calling her back to clean the mess but she'd gotten the better of him and he couldn't help but put her in her place, even if he knew she didn't belong there.

Chapter Five

Cara avoided Jack for the next three days; she cooked, cleaned his house and did his laundry. She left his meals prepared in the oven every night and went straight to her room before he got home. If Julie set him a place at the dining room table or brought his meal to him in his study every evening then he could ring Julie and ask her to come back sooner. She would stay here for one month, she would do everything required of her but she would not spend any unnecessary time with him. She'd thought long about that kiss and concluded that Jack enjoyed seeing her as a play thing, he would get a wakeup call when he realised she may have to change his bed but she would never warm it for him.

She had a gig this evening and she wasn't going to miss it; despite living under his roof. Looking at herself in the long walled mirror Cara was happy with her appearance. She decided on a tight simple blue dress that hugged her curves in all the right places, she straightened her hair and put on more make-up than usual. She wanted to feel good up on the stage that night and not like a frumpy house cleaner. She slipped her feet into her black stilettos and pulled on her black leather jacket as she made her way to the front door.

Jack was exhausted. He slept very little over the last few nights, his body constantly hard thinking about Cara a few doors away. He fantasised about breaking down her door and burying himself deep inside her for hours. Cara had avoided him for the past three nights and he was certain he wouldn't get any closer to bedding her if he didn't apologise. He stepped from his elevator into his entrance hall and was stripping off his jacket and scarf when Cara waltzed past him; dressed to kill. Jack stared speechless as she completely ignored him except for the slight raise of her chin indicating she knew of his presence.

His eyes travelled the length of her body from her long shapely legs right up to her skin-tight dress and darkened eyes. She looked like she was out to impress and he had the sudden urge to lock her up. She didn't look like the Cara he knew, if she hadn't been carrying her guitar case, he might have thought it was a stranger in his home.

"Where are you going?" he asked sheepishly, knowing he had no right to.

"I have a gig, I have a key code. I get a night off, right?" she turned to answer before opening the door to leave. Jack cleared his throat "Yes" he said not sure how to respond to her, she shocked him, *again*.

"Great" she smiled and continued on with her night, leaving him to spend another night alone in his bed.

***

New York City was a scary place for a female to be alone at night. There was a man on every corner wolf whistling and hollering "beautiful" or "hey baby" at any woman with a pulse. In New York you didn't have to be especially beautiful to get that kind of attention, but it often became insufferable and even intimidating on occasions. Cara was no stranger to the men who lurked around every bend just waiting on the next woman they could harass, she kept her head down as she made her way to the subway after her gig. She had stayed on for two drinks and was feeling a little light headed but she kept her wits about her as she headed down the steps to the platform. Her train was due in five minutes, which meant no waiting. As Cara turned the bend she was confronted with a woman about the same age as Mae, being mugged not far from where she was. In a split second she went from being frozen to the spot to running straight at the guy who was grabbing at the woman's handbag.

"Hey!" she yelled as she approached. "Leave her alone." People walked past, ignoring someone in need but Cara couldn't stand by and do nothing.
New York was dangerous so maybe she shouldn't get involved but she felt people should look out for each other more. The man, who hadn't bothered to even wear a mask and who was definitely high on drugs didn't even flinch at Cara's arrival. She began to pull with the woman on her handbag strap. The force caused the strap

to snap and both ladies fell on the ground holding the purse.

"Stupid bitches" he spat before he ran off.

Shaken now and breathless Cara looked at the woman. "Are you okay?"

"Yes, thank you so much" the woman began to cry "I have my wedding ring in here, I couldn't lose it for the world, my husband passed away last year" she stood wiping tears from her face.

Cara hugged her and suggested they go get a coffee together.

They decided not to call the police, there was no point, all it meant was hours of sitting in a police station without the guy ever being caught. They sat for two hours, both filling up on caffeine to calm their nerves and chatting about their lives. The lady was Vanessa; she was living in New York twenty years and hated it. Cara found herself sharing details about her life with this woman and vice versa. They swapped numbers and promised to keep in touch.

"Cara" Vanessa called to her before she stepped into a taxi "If you are ever in trouble and need help, anything, call me."

Cara smiled and hugged her again. She watched Vanessa's taxi pull away and hailed her own cab, just to be on the safe side.

***

Jack didn't like this; he wasn't going to put up with it. As soon as she got home he would be telling her that she was free to come and go as she pleased but as long as she was here for the next month, she would be home at a respectable hour. He was in work the next day and he didn't need to be worried about his half-dressed house-keeper running all over New York in the middle of the night.

He watched her from the top of the staircase, under the cover of darkness, as she removed her high heels once safely inside. She looked tiny as she tiptoed through the living room. She looked so concerned about disturbing him; which for him was laughable, considering he had been disturbed from the moment he met her. "You look like you had a good night" he said as she crept up the stairs.

"Holy crap" she yelped as she jumped back holding her chest "are you trying to give me a heart attack? Why are you sneaking around like that?" she said, her breathing ragged from the fright.

"I'm not the one sneaking in at all hours, that's you" as usual he looked annoyed. Cara was wondering if there was ever any other emotion that flitted across his face, when she noticed him for the first time. Her eyes widened and desire pooled instantly in her belly, he was wearing nothing but a pair of grey cotton bottoms that hung low just above his groin. Her eyes roamed back up and over his hard, toned abs. His sallow skin looked soft and she longed to curl her fingers into his dark chest hairs. With his arms crossed his muscles looked sculpted; he stood defiantly like an authoritative Adonis.

"Well, don't stand there with wide eyes acting all innocent" Jack's voice broke through her erotic thoughts and it amused her that she had, in that moment, been anything but innocent. Cara met him at the top of the stairs. "I'm sorry I'm so late, I helped a lady in the subway and we went for a coffee, we were both a little shaken up." She never imagined that Jack would be waiting up for her.

"What do you mean you helped a lady?"

"Well she was being mugged, so I intervened to.. ."

"YOU WHAT!?!" His voice echoed throughout the condo, causing her to jump again.

"WHY ARE YOU SHOUTING AT ME?" she screamed matching his volume.

"CARA, please tell me you did *not* try to stop an attacker?" his eyes bore into hers.

"Of course I helped her, she was being attacked. What was I supposed to do? Keep walking?"

"YES." Jack turned away and began pacing in front of her, cursing under his breathe.

"Would *you* have walked away Jack?" she tried to make him see sense.

"Don't be ridiculous Cara it's different and you know it is."

"Men are stronger than women, I know that but I also know that two men walked by a woman being mugged and I couldn't do it. Right or wrong I helped, and I would do it again"

"God you are so stupid, you have Mae to think about and here you are with your body on display running around New York acting like super girl."

"Listen! If I 'm anyone I'm Catwoman. I could look good in latex, plus she's got a whip." Cara giggled, she wasn't sure where this was coming from, but in truth she was exhausted and just wanted to lighten the mood.

"Latex? Whips? I think you are trying to change the subject Cara but this one is just as dangerous as the last."

"Well I know how to handle myself, Mr. Cooper" she cocked her brow.

"Ah and how would you handle me?" he moved closer again and into her personal space.

"You don't scare me Jack" Cara stepped towards him and placed her hand on his chest. She felt empowered as she tested him and herself.

"Catwoman would have used her whip on me by now" he teased.

"Oh really? I bet you would just love that" she laughed.

"I'm not into all that but I can't deny the thought of you as Catwoman is pretty sexy."

Cara wasn't sure if it was the shock from that evening or the alcohol in her system but she leaned forward and kissed his chest. Every fibre of her being wanted to do it since he appeared from the shadows. She felt his chest rise and fall, and heard a groan pass his lips.

He grabbed her wrist and pulled her into his room with such speed that before she knew it his door was closed, she was in his arms and his mouth was on hers. She felt his leg move between hers as she steadied herself in his arms, her hands moved up his strong arms and wrapped around his neck holding him to her. His kiss was long and passionate; it was deep and sensual one moment then soft and romantic the next. She knew she couldn't walk away from him tonight. She needed him. She needed to feel him inside of her, so she silenced all the reasons why this was a bad idea. Cara would for once be reckless and take what she wanted, the only person she would hurt would be herself. Her eyes were open to what lay ahead but she dived in nevertheless.

Jack kneeled down before her; starting at her ankles he slowly slid his hands up her legs and under the hem of her dress, never breaking eye contact. Gently he teased the dress higher revealing her black lace underwear. He traced light kisses over her stomach, as he stood, he pulled the dress over her head, disposing of it on the floor.

"You're stunning" he whispered, his voice laced with desire. Cara reached up running her hands through his hair, pulling his mouth to hers desperate to taste him again. Her head fell back and he continued to kiss down her neck causing a moan to escape her mouth. "Jack" she whimpered.

His hands dropped lower as he skimmed the top of her panties, Cara pushed against him urging him to go deeper. Denying her request she felt him smile against her shoulder as he proceeded to remove her underwear. The clasp of her bra came away and the full weight of her breasts fell into his hands. He was a master of seduction and she was desperate for relief, her body burned for his touch. He dipped low taking her hardened nipple in his mouth, sucking at first then biting a little before moving on to the other. She opened her eyes when his warm body left hers to see him remove his cotton trousers; revealing his long, thick manhood. His eyes roamed her body and she felt alive.

"Do you want this?" he asked serious and looking a little nervous. Cara couldn't speak so she nodded and stepped forward taking him in her hand, stroking his arousal. Jack grabbed her head and began kissing her with a renewed force, his hands moved from her hair and down her body as he cupped her ass, lifting her from the ground and walking to his bed. The passion between them was palpable as he shifted between her legs, settling himself at her entrance. She was ablaze with need and yearned for him to push further connecting them completely. Her hips jerked upwards and he answered her call without hesitation; his thickness filling her as she wrapped her legs around his back. Jack leaned on his elbows and looked down into her eyes, all thoughts fell away as their bodies moved together; the intensity growing. Thrusting deeper he pushed her body to new heights of pleasure as they climaxed.

Jack woke the next day with Cara's long hair sprawled across his pillow. Her naked back was exposed, her body covered just to the waist by the white sheet. She looked so peaceful that Jack decided not to disturb her. He needed to talk to her about last night but it could wait until later, for now he would leave her a note.

***

The winter sun broke through the curtains and began to rouse Cara from her sleep. She stretched her body and sighed feeling loose and relaxed. It took a moment for her to remember the night before, memories flooded her mind and she froze in the bed, afraid to turn and find Jack staring at her. Pulling the sheet to cover her chest Cara turned and was relieved to find the bed empty. Sitting on the pillow was a folded piece of paper with her name on it, she smiled reaching over to read the message he left for her. She fell back on the pillow and blinked twice, before reading the note again.

Cara,
Last night was great.
Can you change the sheets today?
Talk later,

Jack

Cara bolted upright in the bed, *that asshole* she screamed inwardly *oh I'll change his sheets alright* she continued as she leapt up, still naked, and began to pull the garments from the bed. She would continue on in her role of perfect house slave but he was laughed at if he thought he would ever get her between his fresh sheets again.

Jack thought about Cara all day and felt a ping of excitement as he approached his front door that evening. She was amazing last night and he was hoping for an encore.
He felt a sense of male pride after having claimed her but she left him wanting more. They'd only touched on how good it could be between them and he throbbed now thinking of all the things he would do to her later. He stepped into the lift and buzzed at seeing her again. The sudden realisation that he had never before come home to a lover shook him, he liked it. He always planned to bed Cara and have Julie back the next day but he needed to rid himself of this primal instinct to make her body his again. He needed to sate his appetite for her before he would let her walk away.
The house was very quiet when he arrived home, the lights were off and it seemed as if Cara had gone out. He walked into the kitchen and smiled when he seen a silver dinner dish. There with a note folded on top with his

name. His smile faded quickly when he read its
contents:

Bed changed and dinner served SIR!
I have retired for the evening.

THE HELP.

What?! Jack blew out a breath *why would she leave a
note like this?* Baffled, he retraced his steps, then it hit
him *the sheets.*
He crumpled the note and rolled his eyes *women!* He
picked up his dinner and headed to his study *why must
everything be so complicated?* He was not about to go
apologising for asking her to do what she was here to do,
he had put the niceties in the note and even said they
would talk later so why would she have to focus on the
negative. Jack opened his laptop and buried himself into
his work; he refused to entertain her childishness any
further.

Cara heard Jack coming home, she waited, hoping he
might have the decency to apologise but upon hearing
the study door close, she knew he really didn't care
about offending her. She made an adult decision the
night before to sleep with him and in that moment, it was

what she wanted more than anything. Their lovemaking brought her to a dizzying ecstasy that she'd never felt, it ripped through her body leaving her shattered and exhausted. It was not something she would forget easily and it pained her to think she might never feel it again. Turning in her bed, she stared up at the ceiling, frustrated and annoyed at how cold Jack Cooper was. He tormented her with his cruel rejection so soon after such an amazing experience and she tormented herself rerunning it all through her head.

He was not the kind of man she wanted to invest in emotionally, he had heart break written all over him. She struggled on throughout the night; in one moment imaging the events of the night before and suffering butterflies and in the next wanting to kick down the study door and give Jack Cooper a piece of her mind. She only had three more weeks left to go, she could get through them if she kept her wits about her and remained calm. Relief washed over her knowing she would soon be home with Mae and when the time came to leave she could walk away and never have to see him again. She would continue on in a professional manner and not let him know how annoyed and hurt she felt.

***

Cara kept the promise she made to herself and became the world's greatest housekeeper to Jack. They remained aloof with each other, like two strangers sharing the same space. She spent her mornings visiting Mae, then made her way back across town to do her work and prepare dinner for Jack in the evenings. Her music was suffering and she wanted nothing more than to take out her guitar and play. She set aside some time that afternoon to start practicing again. Losing herself in her music soothed her soul and right now living with Jack, while he was practically ignoring her, was making her feel lonely and isolated, and writing some songs was exactly what she needed.

Jack was due to attend a fundraising event that evening and came home early to get ready. He knew he wanted Cara to go with him and spent the morning arranging for it to be possible. All he needed to do now was convince her to go; knowing how stubborn she was, he suspected it wasn't going to be easy.
They had barely spoken since that night together and his body was aching to have her again. He hated caving but if he wanted to rid himself of this intense attraction to her, he would have to grow tired of her first. He listened for a few moments outside her door before he knocked; she was singing.

Cara was disrupted from her playing when Jack knocked and immediately entered. Like always when he was around her, she felt herself tremble a little.

"Sorry to interrupt, but I need you to get ready, we have a fundraiser tonight."

Cara sat up straight on the bed, his smell teased her senses as he moved closer. With his height and charisma he commanded the space and his unexpected, powerful presence left her momentarily dumbstruck.

"What fundraiser? I don't want to go to anything like that, besides I don't have a dress" she said her eyes wide with fear, hoping he wouldn't try to force the issue.

"Cara I need a dinner date for tonight's event, Jenny will be here shortly with a selection of dresses, I have arranged appointments for your hair and make-up; so just be ready to go at eight please" Jack's tone was firm but not harsh.

"But Jack, I don't understand, why do you want me to go to it? Surely there are plenty of women you could take?"

"It's part of your job to meet all my needs…" he stopped, his face a little flushed before continuing "… Well, most of them. I would like you there tonight, it makes my life less complicated."

Cara wasn't so sure that she believed Jack, he seemed to be a little anxious. She wanted to put up a bigger fight but he was determined and she knew her attempts would be futile.

"Okay, but strictly business" she warned him. He wouldn't get the chance to bed the hired help again.

"That's exactly how it will be…" he turned to leave but looked back "…for now."

Jack ruffled through his drawers searching for his favourite gold Rolex, he never had trouble finding things when Julie was around. He hated disorder and Cara just rolled his socks up and flung them in with his underwear, his shirts were never pressed the way Julie did them and his sheets were not as soft as when Julie changed them. He thought about all the little added extras that Julie did for him and couldn't wait for her to return. It was great that he didn't find her attractive because he never wanted to lose her as his housekeeper again, in fact he would give her a raise to ensure she stayed on. He was done searching, he would seek Cara out and just ask what the hell she had done with the blasted thing.

He turned to walk towards her room as she walked out and he felt the air being knocked out of him. She was stunning, the most beautiful woman he'd ever laid eyes on. Her hair was swept to the side in a low messy bun, with some soft curls framing her face. She cast dark smoky eyes in his direction and he noticed some hesitation in her step as she moved towards him. The long strapless white evening gown she wore fell to the floor and swayed as she walked. Their eyes met and he was glued to the spot, they both stilled, each silently assessing the other. He found no faults. Her cheeks flushed with colour and her gaze shifted, dipping shyly. Thankful for the break in eye contact, he tried to compose himself *down boy*. He knew he had raked her body with his stare and could see it made her feel a little vulnerable. It was strange for him to feel a wanting to protect her. He realised straight away that Cara Stone was not going to be easy to shake once the affair ended. She had a way of looking like a vixen, a gypsy and a goddess all at the same time and all he wanted to do was undo that dress and stay home.

Cara stood nervously as she watched his eyes travel up and down her body, Jack was not the kind of man to care that he was obviously enjoying the view, he took his time making her feel both delighted and nervous all at once.
"You look…" his eyes roamed her body one more time before he flashed her a side smile and continued with a devilish look in his eyes "…good enough to eat Ms. Stone."
Cara couldn't help but smile and felt her cheeks redden at his innuendo.
"You look handsome" she returned.
Jack wore a black tuxedo with a crisp white shirt, it moulded to his body perfectly. Her mouth watered as she remembered what lay beneath this sexy attire. His dickey bow was undone and hung open around his neck. Her fingers itched to touch him, she wanted to fix his bow-tie and undress him all at the same time. The black leather of his polished shoes glinted in the light and he looked sharp from head to toe. If she was going to be Catwoman then he was definitely her Bruce Wayne.

"Are you ready to go?" she asked.

"Almost, have you seen my Rolex watch? Julie usually leaves it in the top drawer with my cufflinks."

"No, I haven't seen it. Do you want me to help you look for it?"

Cara felt a little uneasy that something so expensive was missing but she knew it must be in there somewhere.

"No it's ok, I'll wear a different one tonight, would you mind looking tomorrow?"

Cara nodded and Jack walked back into his room, she waited by the door for him, taking the opportunity to have one last sneaky glance at herself in the mirror.

***

They travelled in silence to the venue; the air was thick between them making the journey seem longer. Neither had spoken of their night together and Cara was happy to forget the tension between them for tonight. Taking her hand, Jack helped her from the car and her vision blurred instantly as hundreds of flashing lights blinded her. She turned her body towards Jack's and felt his arm tighten around her waist.

"It's ok, just follow my lead" he whispered in her ear causing her to quiver.

Looking up into his hazel eyes she relaxed, his strength and confidence soothed her discomfort and she allowed him to direct her. They smiled and posed for photos for a few moments more before he whisked her inside. The large ballroom was lit up in a warm glow; large candelabras sat in the centre of the many tables strategically placed around the dance-floor. Jack pulled out her chair as they sat, he was being so attentive and sweet and Cara felt her resistance dwindle. He was giving her his full, undivided attention and she lapped it up. He recommended certain dishes, daring her to try new things and she relished every mouth full. The wine flowed between them as they giggled to one another like school kids. The waiters removed their plates as the band began to play and Cara watched as couples took to the floor. She marvelled at how easily they flowed about the room, step by step in sync with each other.

"What are you thinking about?" Jack's fingers skimmed over Cara's as they rested on her lap. The simple touch sent a torrent of lust through her body. She moistened remembering how those fingers had trailed her only nights before. Flashbacks of him wrapped around her had her squirming in her seat. He was looking into her eyes as she swallowed hard, he knew what he was doing, she could see his delight at knocking her off kilter. He wore a mischievous grin that held the promise of a good time.

"Just the couples dancing…" Cara cleared her throat "… I think they look great."

"Would you like to dance Cara?" his voice was low, his eyes captured hers with his and she could only nod as he took her hand and led her onto the floor.

"I'm not very good at dancing" she confessed.

Cara leaned into him, her body drawn to his as he seized her in his embrace. One arm slid around her waist as the other held her hand close to his chest. He stared intently at her as he began to move their bodies as one.

"I'm not very good, I've never danced like this before." she confessed, self-conscious at her clumsy movements.

"What about your prom?"

"I didn't go."

"Why?"

"Nobody asked and besides Mae couldn't afford it so I didn't push it" she shrugged.

"I find it hard to believe nobody asked you…."

"Where did you learn to dance?" she knew it was rude to interrupt him, but Cara felt uncomfortable talking about that part of herself with him. How could a man like him understand what it was like to grow up without money?

"I'm naturally gifted" he smiled and Cara was relieved he let it go.

The night fell away too quickly, Jack twisted and turned her in every direction as they danced and laughed. The music whined down and the band began to pack up for the night. She returned to their table while Jack went to get their jackets. She felt exhilarated and although her feet were swollen she didn't want the night to end. She smiled politely at passing couples as everyone exited the ballroom.

"Let's go" she felt Jack's breath on her neck as he leaned into her back.

"I don't think I can walk" she smiled up at him "I'm sad for the night to end."

"It's not over yet, let's have one last dance"

He looked so boyish as he bent to remove her shoes.

"There's no music" she giggled as he lifted her from the chair, carrying her to the dance-floor.

"I want to hear you sing."

Mortified she tried to pull back but he held her firm in his arms.

"Don't be shy Cara, you have a beautiful voice."

Staff walked about cleaning the tables while she stood in Jack's arms. She had never sang for a man before and it felt so completely intimate. Taking a deep breath she sang the lyrics of her favourite song. Jack bent his head, their cheeks touching as they swayed to her tune. Her voice wavered as he trailed light kisses along her jaw, she was completely distracted and unable to think straight. His lips hovered near hers and she could no longer resist the magnetic pull, she shifted slightly and welcomed the warm and passionate kiss. The staff continued to clean around them as they kissed.

Jack held her close to him as she snuggled into his chest all the way home. It had been a perfect
night and she was totally smitten. Her eyelids felt heavy and she fought to stay awake. She didn't want this night

to end, and she smiled as she dozed off dreaming about their kiss.

Cara roused from her sleep as Jack lifted her from the car, and revelled as she automatically wrapped her arms around his neck. Lucas offered to carry her and Jack was incensed at the idea of another man's hands on her. She was so adorable while she slept and he longed to kiss her again. He pulled her closer as he carried her to his bed inhaling her scent. His body yearned for hers but he resisted waking her up and instead lay beside her fully dressed in his tuxedo and watched her while she slept.

Chapter

Six

Cara awoke with the bodice of her dress digging into her skin the next morning. She blinked against the morning light before realising she was in Jack's bed. She eased her body around gently careful not to disturb Jack, but he was already gone and in his place a note. She had such a wonderful time the night before, that seeing this note tinged her with fear. *Was Jack about to ruin it all again?*

You looked too peaceful to disturb.
Dinner tonight?
Jack

Cara fell back on the pillow smiling, holding the note open over her head she read it once more before giggling. She was enjoying getting to know this side of Jack and although it was risky to invest any emotion, she couldn't stop herself. She was bursting with excitement, she hated having to wait the whole day before seeing him again. Her plans that morning were to visit with Mae before meeting Vanessa for a coffee. She was looking forward to seeing Vanessa again, and finding out how she was since the attack. Anxious to start her day so it could be over she leapt up, full of beans and moved to her room to get dressed. Humming to herself Cara danced about as she got ready, she was checking the time on her phone when she remembered Jack's watch was missing. She could spare ten minutes now to have a scout about, surely it couldn't have gone too far?

The watch was nowhere to be seen and Cara decided to postpone the search for now. She was just about to leave when the elevator doors opened to reveal David.

"Hi Cara, you look fabulous! I just need to collect some papers that Jack left behind" he smiled. Cara had warmed to David the first time she met him, she loved his outgoing personality. He was true to himself, right down to what he wore. She looked at today's trendy choice of clothing and as always admired his bold style. He wore a pale blue shirt tucked into tan chinos. His dark grey tweed jacket and floral dickey bow, along with his large black spectacles, tied the geek chic look together perfectly.

"No Problem, how are you?"

"Great, very busy at the moment and Jack is breathing down my neck, you know how he is" he winked.

"Oh yes I do, I don't envy your job that's for sure."

"I saw some very interesting photos of you and the boss in the papers this morning" David teased.

"All part of the service" she stepped aside to let him in.

"I don't know what service you're providing, but whatever it is, keep it up. I complain about Jack but he isn't half as cranky since you moved in."

"Anything I can do to make your day easier, just holler." Cara laughed as she reached to hold the lift doors.

"Oh I will, and don't you forget who paved the way!" David kissed her cheek before they parted and Cara went about her day. As she sat on the subway to Mae's she felt her phone vibrate in her pocket. A huge smile spread across her face as she read:

Morning, hope you slept ok?

She quickly tapped her reply.

Hi, slept like a baby thanks.

She checked her phone every few seconds eager for his reply and was tickled pink when his name appeared on her screen again.

Dinner tonight?

Cara felt her stomach flip.

Sounds great, what time should I be ready for? I searched for your watch, couldn't find it :/ I'll look again later.

Thanks, what if we stay home? I'll bring some take away and wine?

Trying to keep me cooped up Mr. Cooper?

Just looking out for New York… You tend to get into mischief when you're out there ;)

I can get into just as much mischief at home ;)

Is that right? ;) I'll see you at 8… Catwoman.

Sexy bastard she thought to herself and popped her phone back into her pocket without replying; after all, she didn't want to appear too eager.

***

Mae was looking better every day and Cara was overjoyed to see her up and about. She had a new zest for life and wanted to get back out into the world. Cara managed to convince her to take it easy for a little longer, just to be safe. Ann, Mae's nurse, joined them for lunch, it was obvious that Mae and Ann had formed a close bond and it eased Cara's conscience about not being here. She hugged them both goodbye before meeting Vanessa a few blocks away for coffee. Cara revelled in the few moments she had alone to fantasise about Jack as she walked to the coffee shop. She would need to get home with enough time to shower, pick out some sexy lingerie and get dressed before he got home.

Vanessa was waiting at a small round table just behind the door when Cara arrived. She was a similar age to Mae, but Cara often found kindred spirits of all ages. They hugged like they had known each other for years, and settled into a conversation much the same.

***

Jack picked up a pizza and his favourite bottle of wine on his way home. He sat impatiently tapping his foot in traffic. Cara caught him off guard with her flirty replies earlier and he was anxious to continue where they left off the night before.

Lucas parked the car a few minutes later and he was inside the elevator, making his way up to her in no time. His mind raced all day as he fantasised about Cara, there was something about her that drew him in; it was exciting. The living room and kitchen were empty when he arrived so he decided to pop the pizza in the oven and go find her.

Cara stood frustrated in front of her long mirror. She had no idea what to wear for a dinner date at home. She was still in her towel and her hair dripped wet down her back. Jack had arrived home a few minutes ago and she was running late. She heard a light tap on her door and through the mirror seen Jack. He leaned into the room; one hand on the door handle, the other grabbing the frame. His green eyes met hers in the mirror before she turned to face him. The sexual tension and innuendos from earlier that day rose to the surface. He, like no other man, thrilled and excited her so much so, that she was ready to combust just looking at him. Unsure how it happened, Cara felt the towel slip away from her body, revealing her naked form to him. She found a confidence in that moment, she never knew she had.

Jack crossed the room in two strides, kissing her with the same urgent need to possess that she felt. Stepping away from her momentarily he looked her over once more before groaning and pulling her wet body against him again. Her mind raced as his hands caressed and worshiped her naked body. Reaching for his shirt she freed it from his slacks before aggressively ripping it open and kissing down his hard, toned stomach. Her hand dipped into his boxers desperate to feel and taste him. His erection pulsed in her hands as she held him, dropping to her knees she took him in her mouth. A lascivious need to possess him consumed her as her tongue swirled around his arousal. Fire burned deep in her own stomach as she listened to his groans of pleasure spurring her on, taking him deeper and sucking harder. She looked up as Jack threw his head back almost coming undone in her mouth; he reached for her, fervidly kissing her. Ridding himself fully of his clothes, he cupped her ass lifting her up into his arms, her legs wrapping around his back as he walked to the bed.

"You're so sexy" he murmured bringing her higher up his body, his hot mouth closing over her nipple, nibbling gently. Cara's body was in serious danger of overheating. Jack sat at the edge the bed taking her down with him, kissing her as she settled on his lap. She manoeuvred herself; easing onto him in one slow, deliberate move. Rocking gently, allowing her body time to adjust to his large penis, she threw her head back displaying her breasts for him. Reading her body he once again feasted upon them, his hands caressing her between her thighs as she pushed harder against him. She was close to her pinnacle point when Jack stood, still inside her, and lay her on the bed. "Not yet" he smirked, torturing her as he kneeled before her, lifted her legs around his shoulders and circled his hips slowly, drawing out her pleasure. "Oh Jack" she cried in pleasure as he picked up pace pumping harder, rubbing her as her legs came around his waist again. His head dropped, his tongue teasing her around her nipple before biting it, causing her to explode. Her body shook, as wave after wave of sheer electrifying pleasure raked her, and he thrust twice more before joining her in ecstasy.

Jack looked down at her "Hey" he smiled.

"Hey" she giggled back as he rolled over pulling her against him, his fingers lightly running along the curve of her waist. They lay there in the afterglow of their climax for a few minutes before Jack remembered the pizza.

"I left the pizza in the oven."

"Yum, I'm starved."

"Put on some clothes..." Jack stopped leaned forward and kissed her before continuing "...not too many, I'll meet you in the study."

Cara admired his fine ass as he walked butt naked to the kitchen. She dragged herself out of the bed and feeling a little risky stepped into his boxers and shirt before following him.

They sat on the floor of Jack's study as the fire blazed in front of them, eating pizza and drinking wine. The night fell away as they talked about everything and nothing. The easy flow of wine and conversation made Cara giddy and she found herself moving to his lap. She couldn't get close enough and he welcomed her, kissing her and playing with her hair while they chatted. Jack had managed to wipe the floor with any other date she had ever been on; he knew how to woo a woman. Turning her body to straddle him, he began his slow ministrations over her body again before lowering her in front of the fire to taste all of her. They made love once more in the study before Jack carried her to his bed, still hungry for more of her.

***

Jack woke the next morning to find his bed empty *where had Cara fallen asleep?* He almost missed the note resting on her pillow as he sat up to get ready for his day. He grinned as he read her cheeky note;

Your snoring woke me so

I decided to take the day off and visit my Aunt ....

Could you strip the bed? I'll wash the sheets when I get home

Cara x

Jack dragged himself out of bed and began his day. He was running late again as he searched for his gold cufflinks. His house was upside down and it took him at least an extra ten minutes every morning between, ironing his shirts again, to finding his keys, to un-balling odd socks. He reached for some now, sending up a silent prayer that they matched, the last thing he wanted to do, for the third time this week, was race around looking for a sock.

Mae and Cara spent the morning watching old romantic movies. Their favourite was Casablanca and they swooned as always when Humphrey Bogart came on the screen. Cara missed living with Mae, but her time at Jack's was almost over. She would be back here in two weeks, picking up where she left off, it was a bittersweet thought. When the movie ended, Cara confided in Mae about her relationship with Jack. It lifted a weight off her shoulders, just to say out loud her concerns about the upcoming end to her stay.

Mae walked her to the door when she was leaving and pulled her in for a hug;

"Cara, please be careful" her voice trembled. Cara pulled back shocked to see Mae a little weepy.

"Oh Mae" Cara bent to hug her once more "I'll be fine" she tried to reassure her.

"I don't want you to get hurt, please protect yourself."

"I promise, I really like him and I think he likes me, we just need to talk it over" she smiled.

Your time is coming to an end. I won't allow this to continue for much longer. Soon you will beg for mercy.

Cara looked over her shoulder as she walked into Jack's condo; she had an eerie feeling someone was watching her. A chill ran down her spine, and she pulled her jacket a little tighter. The elevator doors parted and she was greeted with the sound of 80's music coming from the dining room. Cara could see a black garment bag hanging on the door as she approached; it had a note with her name on it

Miss Cara Stone ,

Will you go to prom with me?

I'll pick you up in ten minutes.

Jack

Cara giggled when she unzipped the bag to reveal a hideous pink prom dress. She took it to her room to put it on and laughed harder in the mirror when she seen the finished result. It had large short poof sleeves, the bodice was made of polyester and the skirt was just layers upon layers of tulle that fell to her knees. Cara decided to leave her hair down but quickly applied some blue eye shadow and pink lipstick to complete the look. She was cringing at herself in the mirror when she heard a knock on her door. Jack was really being a true gentleman this evening as he waited for her to answer. She almost hit the floor laughing when she seen him standing there in a blue suit with a white ruffled shirt holding an Orchid corsage. He also looked embarrassed to be making such a big gesture and Cara just wanted to hug him. "You look very handsome" she smiled linking his elbow as he escorted her to the dining room. She stood shocked for a moment taking in, the disco ball and strobe lighting that lit up the room in an array of colours. There was a punch bowl and snacks on a table and Cara just turned to Jack in awe "I don't know what to say, this is amazing. Thank you Jack" she reached up and kissed his cheek.

"It's nothing just some fun, you said you missed your prom" he shrugged and Cara noticed him blushing.

"You do know I was only born in the 80's so this is all before my time" Cara eyed him playfully "but it is exactly the kind of prom I dreamed about" she finished not wanting to sound harsh.

"So why didn't you go to your prom?" he queried

"Oh God this is embarrassing, well firstly nobody asked me and if they had, I probably would have said no" she felt her face heat.

"Why would you have said no?" Jack took Cara's hand and led her to the middle of the room to dance. She buried her face in his shoulder to avoid having to look at him. It was hard to explain to someone like Jack about financial struggles without sounding like you want or expect something from them. She would be truthful, because that was the only way she knew how to be and she hoped he would see it for what it was

"Well Mae worked so hard to provide for me, after she took me in I always felt indebted to her. She was, still is, my hero. I never wanted to take more than she could give and proms are expensive" she smiled wanting to keep it light hearted.

"Cara, can I ask what happened to your parents?" Cara stiffened.

"Well it's a long story… did you go to prom?" she tried dodging the question.

"Not so quick, I will let you ask me any question you like if you tell me your story" Jack winked still playful but Cara feared the night would take a nose dive when she relived her past.

"Jack it's not a pleasant story, don't you want to know who my first kiss was or my favourite colour maybe?" she pouted her eyes wide.

"Yes I do, I want to know all those things, I want to get to know all of you Cara, the good times and the bad." Cara was the most uncomfortable she had ever been in Jack's company, though there was a part of her that felt at ease opening up to him, she'd never confided this story with anyone other than Mae and the police, but that was a very long time ago.

"When I was a little girl my Dad, Matthew, passed away suddenly of a heart attack. I was seven years of age and I remember it like it was yesterday. He was my world, he was a musician" Cara looked up at Jack with sheer admiration and sadness in her eyes. "Anyway" she continued "my mom was devastated, she was so beautiful, so naturally beautiful, she attracted a lot of men, some nice, some not so nice. She didn't sleep around or anything but I think she was trying to fill the huge void my Dad had left. I remember listening to her cry every night, she obviously thought I was sleeping. She started seeing this one guy Rodney Winters, one night when I was nine, he came into my room and…" Cara felt Jacks arms tighten around her back "I'm sorry, I shouldn't be telling you this, it's just that I wanted to explain."

"Cara" he spoke, his tone laced with sympathy "It's ok, continue" he encouraged her.

"He tried to get me to kiss him and I called my Mom, that's what little girls do right? They call their Mom or Dad when they're afraid. I won't ever forget the look of terror in her eyes when she seen him on my bed, he was so big and muscly. The look changed almost instantly to rage and she came running over, screaming and yelling at him to get out or she would call the cops. It all happened so quick, one moment he was getting ready to leave then she said the word cops and he flipped, the next thing he was hitting my Mom. I tried to help her but he pushed me away so I ran for help, but…" Cara began to sob "…he killed her Jack" she cried.

Jack held her as she wept and she welcomed the feeling that he cared.

"I am so sorry that you went through that Cara."

Cara was too embarrassed to look up at him just yet. She was sure she looked a fright.

"I'm sorry I got so upset, I can go days, weeks even, without thinking about it but it has been a long time since I spoke of it."

"Did they ever catch him?"

Jack was still holding her tight and she allowed herself to feel protected and cared for, it felt good.

"Yes, he was sentenced to twenty five years in prison, but they let him go a few months ago. He only served twenty years."

Cara refused to think about him free in the world, she would not live her life filled with anger or fear.

"You are very brave."

Jack was about to explode with anger. The thoughts of what Cara had to endure enraged him to the point where it took every fibre of his being to remain calm and try support her. The last thing she needed after telling a story like that was a man losing his temper. He looked down at a mass of wavy blonde hair as she snuggled into his chest and wondered how anyone could survive such traumas in their lives and grow up to be as talented and smart as she was. Jack lifted her chin and looked into her eyes before he began to gently kiss her wet cheeks "you're okay, I'm here" he whispered as he moved to her lips and dipped his tongue softly into her mouth massaging it with hers. Her body melted against his as they fed off the others strength, turning the mood from sombre to lustful. Jack wanted this night to be fun for her so he turned up the music and twirled her around the dance floor until she was dizzy with laughter. After a few minutes he was delighted to see her enjoying herself again.

***

Jack paced his office the next day; his hair was a mess from constantly running his hands through it. He had woken up that morning and left Cara another note. He had been playful and charming in it and right now he hated himself. He didn't want this to get out of control and yet he couldn't help but immerse himself in her, she was the only woman who ever made him laugh, or angry or anything other than numb. He never dived head first into any of his conquests, female or business and he felt like he was losing himself. He would need to rein himself in and remind Cara that he is not the settling down kind of guy. He liked her company and enjoyed their love making but right now the line between lovers and a relationship were blurred. He would need to pull back a little and speak with her about ending the affair once Julie returned. He relaxed back at his desk determined to set some boundaries that evening when he got home. He laughed recalling the message he had left her that morning:

Good Morning Sexy x
I'm already looking forward to seeing you later.
Get that fine ass out of my bed and scrub this place ;)

Cara had purposely not text Jack all day; she wanted him to miss her. His note that morning had made her giggle and she decided she would play a little trick of her own on him, when he got home. She watched out the window for his car to arrive and then hid in the hallway waiting for him to come home.

The hallway was in darkness when Jack stepped inside, but it lit up immediately causing his eyes to be dazzled for just a second as an object came at his head with too much speed to deflect it in time.
"Whoa! What the hell are you doing?" he yelled, baffled as he watched Cara fold her arms stick up her chin and scuttle towards her room. Jack looked down on the floor and seen his note from that morning in a ball at his feet and he began to laugh as he rushed after her.

Cara felt strong arms come around her waist as Jack lifted her from the ground "It was a joke crazy woman" he laughed as he carried her into his bedroom. She wriggled and cursed in mock indignation for him to release her, but instead he kissed her neck and whispered how sexy she was all the way to the bed. She was putty in his hands by the time he turned her around to face him and she couldn't help but giggle. "Gotcha" she laughed. She watched as realisation dawned on him "I should have you arrested for assault" he teased as he threw her down onto his bed.

"Please don't Sir, I'll make it up to you" she faked sincerity as she kneeled, crawling to the edge of the bed where he stood.

"How do you plan to do that?"

Cara slid his red tie through her fingers before tugging it, pulling him to her and kissing him with just as much force as she used to throw the note at his head.

The next morning Cara woke up to another note:

Good morning sexy...

I wonder what punishment you will have in store for me if I told you to empty the bins today?

Jack was sitting with David running through his morning's schedule when he heard his phone vibrate and seen Cara's name flash on the screen. He smiled as he opened the message from her:

Memo received Mr. Cooper, I will be waiting for you tonight, to empty them over your head! I know you like it dirty ☺

Jack laughed out loud when he read Cara's message, the little minx knew how wind him up.

David sat across from Jack in complete awe; firstly at seeing his boss stop in a meeting to read and laugh at what was clearly a personal text and then at how white and perfect his smile was. If he could give himself a pay rise he would, clearly the French maids outfit had done the trick.

Cara was exhausted, between running Jack's house, visiting Mae and spending her nights in Jack's arms she felt ready to drop. She woke every morning in his bed, a little note waiting for her. He was mostly funny but sometimes he would write something short and sweet like "have a good day."
She hadn't emptied the bins over his head a few nights before, instead she had tried to cook him a nice meal. The chicken had been a little burnt and not fully cooked through. It had delighted Jack and he spent the rest of the night mocking her ability in the kitchen. Cara smiled at how her abilities in the bedroom hadn't elicited any complaints so far. She was sitting on the subway, returning home from Mae's when he messaged her:

I'm guessing the dinner will either be burnt or on the floor when I get home, take out?

Yeah... I have many skills but cooking is not one of them Mr. Cooper ;)

Yesterday morning, Jack left a note demanding the floors be cleaned. She had been a great housekeeper and was in the middle of polishing them when he arrived home. The apartment was very warm all day so she wore the little French maids outfit to help keep her cool. She suppressed her laughter on the subway as she remembered Jack's face when he walked in to find her naked beneath the flimsy costume and kneeling over, pretending to wipe the floors.

"How does it look?" she had winked.

"I could eat of those floors.... In fact, I think I will." They had made love right there in his hallway. Their need for each other too great to wait until they got to the bedroom.

Her phone buzzed again bringing her out of her daydream.

Don't I know it! I'm lucky to be alive… you will need to refresh my memory on these other skills later ;)

Oh I don't doubt that you have been rerunning my skills in your mind all day... Do you do any work?

Is that right? Maybe I'll show you exactly what I've been thinking about when I get home… try not to burn down the house before I get there ;)

Cara smiled as she popped her phone back into her pocket and prepared to get off at the next stop. She still had to do a full day of work at Jack's. Despite the fact that they were sleeping together and having fun Cara was still there to repay a debt. She paused for just a moment wondering if Jack had planned this all along, and then wiped those thoughts from her mind. Jack had all but hated her at the beginning, there was no way he planned any of this. The truth was that even if he had, she would never know and she was having fun and choosing to continue it, if it all went belly up she would deal with it then.

Cara arrived home a little later and instantly felt uneasy. She paused just inside the hall, looking around the living area. It was hard to explain how she was feeling, her entire body was on edge, her intuition was screaming don't go any further. She moved a little further into the house making her way to the kitchen, she called out Jack's name to make sure he wasn't there but got no reply. There was an eerie stillness and Cara decided to investigate further. She removed a knife from the chopping block, before making her way back to the living room and up the stairs. She looked back down the stairs, frozen to the spot before scolding herself for being so silly *it's my imagination* she repeated like a mantra as she walked to her room first. Her door was slightly ajar causing a flurry of nervousness to wreak havoc once more in her tummy, she was certain she'd closed it that morning. She felt a cold draft as she walked in *maybe the wind blew it open* she hoped. Nothing seemed out of place so she moved on to Jack's room and again the room was empty. She was about to move back downstairs when she noticed his walk in wardrobe was open. Her mind began to go into overdrive as she pictured a crazed psycho waiting behind the door, she walked quickly over, afraid she might lose her nerve and found it to be empty. Jack's jewellery draw was open, as she was closing it a deep male voice caused her to yelp as she jumped around;

"What are you doing?"
Jack was standing at the entrance to his wardrobe with a suspicious look on his face. Cara was a little taken aback at first to register his expression.
 "I'm sorry I came home and thought somebody was in the house, so I was just checking the rooms" she explained, her voice was jittery, she hadn't realised how wound up she'd been. Jack eyed her cautiously and Cara realised he thought she had been up to no good.
"Jack I would never steal from you, I hope you know that" she eyed him right back, reminding him that she was not some stranger anymore.
"Okay, I'm sorry, it was just a bit weird seeing you in here with a knife" he pointed to her hand.
"I will just go put this back" she laughed as she walked past him, heading for the kitchen. Jack grabbed her wrist, gently tugging her against him.
"Cara don't ever enter this apartment again if you think it is dangerous, do you understand?" Cara looked up into dark, intense eyes and nodded. His voice was almost menacing. She pulled back and continued to the kitchen, the exchange between them had been a little strange and Cara felt that Jack somehow doubted her story.

Jack watched Cara descend the staircase to the kitchen and despite every part of him wanting to believe her, he couldn't help but wonder. He was missing some expensive items since she moved in and it didn't help finding her in the cabinet, going through his things, with a guilty look on her face. In spite of wanting to forget the incident he found himself checking his belongings.

"You owe me the answer to one question" Cara smiled across at Jack as they ate lunch.

"I thought I had escaped that one" he grimaced.

"Not on your nelly."

Jack began to laugh at Cara's expression and within a few seconds everything felt normal again.

"Okay Ms. Stone one question, make it count!" he sighed.

"Are you happy?"

Jack was grinning from ear to ear at such an easy question "Yes I am, especially when I'm inside you" he reached over and kissed her long and hard.

Cara pulled away breathless "that's not what I meant, I mean are you happy in life?"

Jack took a deep breath "Cara I'm not in search of happiness, I love my work and I love my life happiness is a fleeting emotion like the rest of them and I'm human so I feel it from time to time" he shrugged his shoulders.

"That is the most idiotic thing I've ever heard" Cara looked at him like he had just stuck his hand into a fire.

"No Cara, I decide how and what and when and where and if I choose to search for everlasting happiness, I'm sure I will be left looking."

Cara began to giggle "Jack you are so cynical, but despite what you say I'm sure you want to be happy."

"Cara I'm happy enough, how about that?"

"Well if that's good enough for you then I suppose that's good enough."

"What about you Little Miss Happy are *you* actually happy?"

"Most days I feel happy, yes, I guess I am, I'm happy with myself and the type of person I am. I know I live my life by my own standards. Money and possessions are not important to me, people like you and Mae are what matter to me" Cara realised that for the first time in her life she felt whole. Mae was on the mend and her and Jack had this wonderful thing blooming between them. She knew she only had nine more days left staying with him and she wanted to make each one count. She felt that Jack connected with her on the same level but there was a very real deep fear that he could pull a Houdini on her. She knew him less than two months and intimately for only two weeks but the little girl who dreamed of happy endings inside of her wanted him to be the one, while the woman in her wanted her to keep her head about her. She was falling head over heels in love with him and she was falling so fast she couldn't reach the brakes. Her heart soared just imagining that it might all work out for them, Jack hadn't indicated otherwise so she believed she had a real chance at happiness with him.

***

The next morning Cara woke up with a stuffy nose and watery eyes, her head felt like it weighed a tonne as she lifted it from the pillow to seek out some medication. She decided to crawl back into her own bed for the day, she would text Jack and request a sick day. She searched his side of the bed for her morning note, but was disappointed to not find anything.

I feel really ill, it's just a head cold but can I take today off? X

It felt wrong now to be still Jack's housekeeper but a deal was a deal and Cara would see it through to the end. She remade Jack's bed and was heading into her own room when she received a reply from him;

I will send David or Jenny over with some soup, take care of yourself. Talk later.

Cara reread the message, everything was as it should be, kind and caring and yet she knew from the core of her that Jack was being distant with her. She couldn't explain it only that something had changed, she thought back to the day before, everything had been fine after lunch. Jack had returned to work but got home later, that was fairly normal enough, except that he hadn't come to find her, she'd gone to him and now she wondered if he would have left her in her own room and not made love to her. Cara was too ill to try and dissect why Jack was pulling back but she fell into a deep slumber hoping that it was just a bad day at the office.

Jenny popped by later that afternoon with soup and bread. Cara looked like crap and felt even worse when she seen Jenny. She waltzed in full of energy and vitality, her skin glowing and her big blue eyes sparkling. Her petite figure was displayed to perfection in cropped beige slacks, a buttoned down white shirt with a mustard jacket and belt pulling the whole ensemble together. *God, all Jack's staff are so stylish* she acknowledge to herself, thinking about David. She chatted with Jenny for over an hour as they ate lunch together, she was so sweet. Cara found out she worked for Jack for almost ten years;

"Is he a pain to work for?" Cara asked giggling, knowing too well he was.

"You should know better than me, I get to go home in the evenings" she winked.

"Well, I get to escape to a beautiful big room" she blushed.

"Oh Julie was not happy about you moving in at all" Jenny laughed.

"Well she must have expected someone would cover her holiday?"

"Yes but usually you pick your holidays, poor Julie is worried she is being pushed out" Jenny continued before noticing the confused look on Cara's face. "What?" Jenny asked perplexed.

"But Jack hired me to cover Julie's holidays... No?"

"Oh right I see, maybe I made a mistake" Jenny was the one who now looked a little embarrassed.

"Jenny you don't make mistakes, just spit it out, why am I here?"

"Look David just told me that Julie wasn't happy about taking the month off at short notice so Jack compensated her for the inconvenience, oh God I have said too much? Jack will fire me for talking out of turn, please Cara don't say a thing" Jenny looked terrified.

"Jenny relax, I promise I won't say a thing, it's not a big deal I'm sure it's a misunderstanding."

Cara knew damn well it wasn't a misunderstanding. Jack arranged for her to live here, not because he was stuck but because he had other plans. It was looking like, she was his live-in sex buddy for thirty nights and her days were numbered. She crawled back into bed when Jenny left worried about the forthcoming days. Was she really just here to service Jack's desires for one month? There was only one way to find out and that meant getting Jenny into trouble. Cara would just pull back and hope that she had it all wrong.

***

Jack came home late that evening, he'd been working late the last two nights, trying to avoid Cara. He needed to decide how he was going to approach her about the missing items and also about the impending end to their agreement. He really liked Cara, she was sexy and sweet and a lot of fun to be around but none of those things would matter if he found out she was stealing from him. He hated liars and she would not walk away with his possessions without him confronting her first. He tried to reason it all out in his mind, the fact that she didn't at all seem to be the type of person to do such a thing was outweighed by the fact that he had only known her for a few weeks and his belongings went missing when she moved in. He decided to leave her alone for the evening and try get some sleep.

Cara listened as Jack shut his bedroom door and cried silently. She knew what was coming and her heart was just not ready for the rejection yet. She tried to understand where it all went wrong and why he was pulling away but all that didn't matter, what mattered was that she was here in his home and now she felt like she was more of a hindrance than a help.

She woke during the night with puffy eyes and a red nose and made her way to the kitchen for some water and more medication. She was rummaging through the medicine cabinet when Jack walked in and flipped the lights on.

"What are you doing?" he asked her, his tone flat and his face red.

Cara looked up from where she was bent into the cabinet "I'm just getting some medicine."

Cara stood when she seen the look on Jack's face. "Why are you looking at me like that?" she asked her heart racing.

"Why are you creeping around in the dark Cara?"

"I didn't want to wake you and there is plenty of light from the hall…why are you looking at me like that Jack?" her voice was croaky from her cold.

"Cara twice in two days I have caught you rummaging through two different cabinets and things are missing so…"

"Things are missing? What things? So, what are you saying? I'm a thief?!" she felt her face heat as rage began to fill her body.

"My watch and cufflinks are missing and I didn't say that you're a thief it just looks suspicious" Jack matched her volume.

"You just said it, how dare you!" Cara took the bottle of pills she was holding and through them at him.

"I was just about to steal these, I figure the street value for paracetamol these days must be pretty high" Jack caught the bottle in his hands.

"It is fair for me to ask Cara, I hardly know you."

Cara gasped "You know me as much as anyone has ever known me in my life you asshole! I opened up to you, trusted you and for what? To be accused of stealing and made to feel disposable!" Tears slid down Cara's face.

"I didn't accuse you Cara" he roared "and we both knew it was coming to an end soon."

Cara looked up into his eyes, tears pooled her vision but she would look him in the eye when she spoke "Oh yes you accused me Jack, you didn't sit me down and explain that you were concerned things were missing. You didn't reassure me that you were just covering all the basis about their possible whereabouts did you? Oh no you see me looking for medication and assume I'm a thief in the night. I might remind you Jack that you're the one who orchestrated for me to be here, you're the one who lied and you're the one who stole from me!"

"What the hell are you talking about?! Don't change the subject."

"I wanted to repay you all the cash that you paid for Mae's operation but you had other ideas, nice to know I was just a glorified hooker for a few weeks."

Jack moved closer to Cara, her body was straight and rigid, her tears had dried; from the heat of her rage. She was wearing a long white nightgown and looked like anything but a hooker right now.

Jack glared down at her "Don't you try and turn this Cara" the muscle in his jaw twitched.

"I hope you find your missing watch and cufflinks Jack, and when you do I want you to know that I hate you for how you have treated me and I hate myself for thinking you were more than the shallow asshole I first met."

Jack grabbed Cara's arms "I want you out of my home."

"With pleasure!" she felt herself go numb to any emotion and stepped back before walking away.

Cara walked straight to her room with Jack on her heels to pack her belongings; she whipped around just as she entered the room "Come to check what I'm packing? Here let me show you." Cara pulled out each drawer one by one and poured them onto the bed.

"Stop this Cara, you can do all this in the morning" Cara was on the second last drawer and looked up at him in sheer disbelief.

"You have got to be kidding, I would rather sleep on the streets, than stay here" she spat.

She haphazardly pulled out the bottom drawer and emptied it on top of all her other clothes. Her eyes widened when she seen what fell out with her clothes. There, on top of her clothes lay Jack's watch, his cufflinks and a money clip with money.

"Jack…I…"

"Don't say another word." Jack walked over to pick up his belongings, his face filled with unspoken fury as he examined them in his hands.

"GET OUT" his voice boomed throughout the condo causing Cara to jump, she grabbed a shoulder bag and stuffed some clothes inside it as quickly as she could. Pulling on jeans and a jumper she turned to Jack who was watching her every move. The shock of what was unfolding hit her and she pleaded one last time praying he would see the truth in her eyes.

"I didn't do this Jack."

"I was actually beginning to feel sorry for you with your pathetic display; if I ever see you again I will have you arrested."

Cara's hand covered her mouth as she gasped at his threat. There was no way for her to salvage this situation so she silently walked away.

Jack watched Cara's shoulders shake, she tried to contain her sobs as she walked out of his home. She looked a fright with her messy hair and pale skin, her face puffy from crying. Jack knew it was wrong to let her go at this hour but his pride would not let him falter. She'd betrayed his trust and he had actually begun to regret ever doubting her. Yes, he was mad that she said she hated him, but he didn't mean it when he told her to get out the first time. He was just about to apologise when the evidence of her thievery appeared. He would call Mae's in an hour and speak with the Nurse to make sure Cara had arrived safely; despite everything he still cared if she was ok and he hated himself for it.

Cara stood outside in the cold crying for twenty minutes before deciding what she wanted to do. Secretly she hoped Jack would come running after her, but she knew it was never actually going to happen. Cara took out her phone, she couldn't face Mae, she didn't want to worry her and she couldn't face the pity. She was a fool and Mae had tried to warn her, she just needed a day or two to figure out how she would explain all this to her. She had no car, no money and very few friends so Cara decided to phone Vanessa. She may not know her very well, but she'd told her that if ever she needed help to phone and that was exactly what she needed right now. A non-judgemental friend.

I knew Jack Cooper would eventually get rid of her! Now that the coast is clear, I can take what is rightfully mine and nothing or nobody can come between us now.

Chapter Seven

Cara arrived at Brookdale Apartments in Queens twenty five minutes later, and looked up from the curb at the red brick building. The complex was about twenty stories high and overlooked the Queensboro Bridge. Cara felt good to be so close to home, but right now she didn't want to worry Mae. She punched in Vanessa's apartment number and was relieved when the buzzer sounded on the door. She stepped out of the cold night and into the warmth of the foyer.

Vanessa's apartment was bright and welcoming. Cara walked through into the living area and admired the cosy feel of Vanessa's home. The walls were taupe with an exposed brick wall on the left which housed a large fireplace and a teaming bookcase. The floors were deep cherry-wood and a green couch was underscored by a large colourful abstract rug.

"Let me take your things into the guest room" Vanessa smiled as Cara handed over her bag.

"I'm so sorry for intruding on you at this hour" Cara was mortified to have put Vanessa out.

"Don't be silly, make yourself comfortable, I'll pop the kettle on."

Cara relaxed into the soft cushions and looked around the small room. This apartment was much smaller than Jacks but it held more charm. The evidence of Vanessa's happy life here came alive everywhere she looked. Photos of Vanessa and her husband were standing proud in gold frames on the mantelpiece. She looked to the right and sitting on the side table was another one of them both on their wedding day. Vanessa was grinning from ear to ear as she looked into her new husband's eyes and he was exactly the same. Cara wondered for just a moment what that would feel like, before her eyes watered up. The rattling of china on the tray Vanessa carried into the room, shook her from her sentimental daydream. They sat for over an hour, Cara filled her in on everything that happened over the last few weeks between her and Jack. Her emotions were playing havoc, she found herself laughing and crying and then filled with angry as she recalled the events of this evening.

Vanessa reached over and placed her hand on Cara's "I'm going to tell you something Cara and I hope it helps…" she smiled warmly rubbing Cara's hand "…When I first met my husband Richard we fell madly in love and married within the year. It was so romantic that first year but when we got married, boy did we fight. Living under the same roof is tough especially when you're in love, you misunderstand each other and go crazy at the other's bad habits. We got through it because what we felt for each other was bigger than the small things that can so easily rip couples apart. If Jack loves you he will see that he was wrong, I have only known you a short time and already I believe you could never do such things, try to have some faith in him."

"I would have thought that too Vanessa but after everything that has happened how could he ever believe it wasn't me?"

"Cara all this started happening when you moved in and you said you felt someone in the apartment…you need to think it through."

Cara wracked her brains trying to figure out who would want to frame her and she came up empty every time.

"There's only David and Jenny who I know have keys but they're so nice, I just could never believe they would do such a thing, plus I'd never dream of accusing them."

"I understand but you can't sit back either and allow him to accuse you."

"Yeah I know but what am I gonna do? He is never going to believe me and I'd rather take care of Mae than run around New York like Sherlock Holmes." Fresh tears escaped and suddenly she felt exhausted.

"Why don't you get some sleep and we can talk it over again tomorrow."

They both hugged goodnight and Cara climbed into the large double bed. Her body enveloped in cotton sheets sank into the soft mattress as sleep over-powered her.

Jack stormed into his office, slamming his door behind him. It was almost three days since anyone had heard from Cara and he wanted to murder her, *if she isn't already dead!* Ann, Mae's nurse was to inform him as soon as she showed up. He stood staring out the window, his mind too preoccupied with where she could be, to work. He had phoned every hospital and police borough for information but it had all been fruitless. She was missing and he was responsible. He hung his head low as he offered up a silent prayer for her safe return.

It was time to face reality and go home to Mae. The last three days at Vanessa's had been exactly what Cara needed to clear her mind and get some perspective on everything. She packed the few belonging she brought with her and came out to have breakfast with Vanessa; "How are you feeling this morning?" Vanessa asked as she lifted pancakes onto some plates. They smelt delicious "Great" she tried sounding upbeat, as she forked some of the fluffy goodness into her mouth.
"So have you decided what you're going to do next?"
"Yes, I'm going to go home and take care of Mae. I already owe Jack a lot of money that I intend to fully repay so taking over Mae's care will lower some of that cost."
"You seem much stronger today."
Cara thought back over to the weeping mess she was the past few days. "Vanessa, I can't thank you enough for being so kind to me."
"That's what friends are for."

***

Cara arrived home later that morning both excited to see Mae and nervous about getting her life back in order. Jack whizzed into her life, turned it upside down and now all she could see was a mess she needed to tidy up.

She stood on the perch for a few minutes, collecting herself. She hated the fact that he left her feeling like something was missing from her life, she had been happy and contended before they met and now she needed to figure out how to move forward without him. With a raging determination to be stronger than she felt right now she turned her key and stepped back into the world she knew and where she belonged.

Ann was sitting on the sofa taking notes in Mae's daily care plan. She looked up when she heard the door close and a smile spread wide across her face.

"The wanderer returns" she winked as she stood up, putting her clip board down on the coffee table.

"Hi, how's Mae?"

"She is doing great, she is just having her afternoon nap."

"That's so good to hear. Thank you so much Ann…"

Cara moved towards the kitchen and Ann followed. They both had developed their own relationship during Cara's morning visits with Mae. Ann was in her early thirties and they had a lot in common, especially their taste in music. Ann had been delighted at Cara's cd collection when she first came to stay. "…coffee?"

"Yes, sounds great".

Ann sat at the small round kitchen table as Cara pottered about preparing the coffee and putting some biscuits out. "Jack has been calling here every day looking for you…" she announced as Cara carried the coffees to the table. Shrugging her shoulders she sat down, unable to make eye contact with Ann. All the reasons he might be looking for her crossed her mind *to have me arrested? To get his money? To say sorry...* she shook her head at that last thought, reminding herself this wasn't a movie script.

"Well I'm under strict orders to inform him as soon as you arrive home."

Cara burnt her tongue on the coffee "ouch" she moaned placing her cup down a little too hard, causing it to slosh over the edges.

"Oh no, not another patient" Ann laughed at her clumsiness.

"Ann, I can't handle seeing him right now ..."

"Cara calm down, Jack Cooper is not my boss... I wanted to tell him where to go, but then I would be in serious trouble with my actual boss, apparently Dr. Roberts was good friends with Jack's father."

"I don't want you to get into trouble Ann, but after today I won't be beholden to Jack anymore." Cara looked at her hands as she knotted them on her lap. Letting Ann go was going to be one of the hardest things she would ever have to do. There was no way she could match the care she provides to Mae and she was also aware of the bond that Mae and Ann had developed.

"Cara it's ok..." she looked up and Ann was smiling fondly at her "... this was always short term. I still have a job at Dr. Roberts's surgery."

"Oh Ann I feel terrible, but I can't allow Jack to continue paying"

"Mae is much better, she is more than capable of taking her medication and really it won't be like before I arrived. You have seen the improvement yourself."

Cara was silent as tears welled in her eyes, she didn't want to cry the bitter sweet tears the threatened to fall.

"Mae will miss you" she finally managed with only one rogue tear managing to get free.

"I hope I will be allowed stop by for coffee every so often, I'm only a few blocks over! Jeez don't completely write me off!!"

They both finished their coffee, the air was clear and Cara's chest felt a little lighter as one weight fell away.

Mae woke up about an hour later and was also sad to see Ann leave but delighted in having her niece back home.

Ann ran through everything with them both about ten times, and insisted they call her if they had any trouble or question.

"I have a few days off now, I think I will visit my parents" Ann smiled as she gathered her bags at the door, waiting on her cab to arrive.

"Oh Ann you should, your Mom will be delighted" Mae encouraged the plans.

The taxi beeped outside and everyone was a little teary eyed as they all hugged goodbye before laughing when Ann reminded them she would be back the following week for coffee.

"WHAT DO YOU MEAN YOU ARE ON YOUR WAY TO WASHINGTON?!" Jack erupted down the phone line the next day.

"MR.COOPER please lowers your tone" Ann warned. Jack took a deep breath and pushed back from his desk in his black leather chair. He felt like he was going mad as he loosened his red tie and opened the top two buttons of his shirt. He was highly stressed and it was all because he had no control over Cara, where she was, who she was with or what she was doing. He was unable to gain any information on her whereabouts almost five days later. *All the money in the world and I can't get hold of one small woman in the same God damn city as me !!* His frustration was affecting his work, and now he was growling down the phone at Mae's nurse.

"I'm sorry, please excuse me. Why are you no longer caring for Mae?"

"Mr. Cooper I'm afraid I can't give a patients information out, what I can say is that someone has taken over in that role and no longer requires our service." If Jack could reach down the phone and shake the information he wanted from her right now, he would seriously consider doing it.

"So is Cara home safe or not?" he asked tired of skirting around what he really wanted to know.

"I'm a nurse Mr. Cooper, my patient's privacy and that of their families is more important than your need for information. I suggest you hire a private detective. I'm officially on annual leave. Good day."

Jack heard the dial tone as Ann hung up on him and flung his phone against his office door. He would need to get confirmation that Cara was home safe and maybe then he could sleep easy.

Cara felt a little bit useless the past twenty four hours. Mae was in great spirits and was more than capable of her own care and as much as it thrilled Cara to see her finally begin to look like herself again, she was worried Mae was pushing herself too quickly. They both decide to snuggle up on the couch and watch a movie and had just sat down when the doorbell rang. Cara peeked through the lace curtains that hung in the window but could only see the side profile of a woman, she didn't immediately recognise, at the door. She pulled open the door, curious about who might be calling at this hour;
"Hi, Ms. Stone is it?" The tall, red haired beauty smiled. Cara's brows knitted together as she tried to figure out how she might know her.
"Yes" she said cautiously.
"I work for Dr. Roberts's surgery, I'm sorry to call so late but I need to confirm that you are now the full time carer for your aunt?" Her red lips pursed slightly as she looked over Cara's shoulder to where Mae was sitting on the couch.
Cara relaxed a little knowing she was a colleague of Ann's "Yes that is correct, do you need me to sign any papers?"

"No that's all I need to know, Thank you have a good evening" she smiled as she eased her way down the steps.

Cara settled back onto the couch only to be disturbed a few minutes later by yet another late caller. Mae paused the movie and they both smiled at each other "Hopefully we get to watch it this century" Mae joked as Cara moved yet again to answer the door. She half expected it to be Dr. Roberts' assistant again but was met with a very different pair of green eyes. Jack was glaring at her and she automatically tried to close the door again. His hand came up, stopping it before she could close it all the way.

"We need to talk" he hissed holding the door without pushing it.

Cara inhaled deeply, closing her eyes for just a moment before she faced him again. Stepping aside allowing him entry, he made his way to the kitchen. Mae watched as they passed her and Cara held up two fingers, indicating she would be two minutes. Closing the kitchen door behind her she kept her voice low;

"What do you want Jack, if you're here for your money I will have it as soon as I …"

"I don't care about the money Cara, where the hell have you been the past five days?" he rasped trying to keep his voice low.

"That's none of your business Jack, I wasn't out ripping innocent people off if that's what you're worried about!"

she ground out through clenched teeth as all the hurt of his accusations assailed her.

"Don't be ridiculous, you can't just disappear like that leaving Mae to worry about you!"

"Since when do you care about who worries about me? I text Mae, she knew to expect me home within a few days!"

"Ann never said…." His eyes narrowing as he realised Ann obviously refused to pass on any information to him.

"That's not her job! Why are you here?"

"To check you got home safe! And to ask why you dismissed Ann?"

"Mae is a lot better she doesn't need round the clock care. We appreciate everything you did Jack; I will repay you over time…"

"I don't care about the damn money, keep it!" he moved to leave, their bodies touching briefly as he passed her. That familiar bolt of electricity shot through her.

"That's right you got paid in kind" Cara shot wrapping her arms around her tummy. It hurt like hell to imagine that it had all been a figment of her imagination. That Jack had used her for sex and like every other woman who entered his life she would be left by the wayside.

"That's not how it was Cara" he spoke softly now from behind her, his hand resting on her shoulder. Stepping forward and out of his touch she decided to finish the charade once and for all;

"Maybe I disappointed you in that regard, maybe you planted the missing items to get rid of me?" she challenged him.

 "You were plenty satisfactory Cara, so good I paid twice" he bit back.

Cara turned quickly and slapped him hard across the face, stinging her own hand in the process. She instantly stood back as his eyes narrowed and his face reddened. Shame washed over her as the hand print appeared on his cheek. She stood shaking as tears slid down her face; her breathing was jagged as she tried to compose herself. She wanted to run from the room, to cry in peace. His eyes bore into hers as they faced each other both raw with so many emotions.

"That's the last time you ever get to touch me" he said with a level of self-control that Cara longed to possess.

"I shouldn't have done that, I'm sorry…" she walked towards the fridge to retrieve an ice-pack.

"Don't bother! I'm going; I will have Lucas bring the rest of your belongings tomorrow."

Cara watched as he whirled around and walked straight through the apartment and out of her life for good.

"So now will you tell me what the hell is going on?" Mae came in a moment later and Cara walked into her arms, hugging her as she sobbed.

She was safe; he had seen her and knew she was back home with Mae. Cara had looked frail and tired with dark circles around her eyes and once again the shame of throwing her out in the cold while she was sick, came to the forefront of his mind. She'd looked ill and all he'd achieved was to upset her further. He couldn't seem to do anything other than upset her. His fists balled as he remembered the hurt in her eyes after his nasty comments, the spark in them had gone out and he was the reason why.

He ground his teeth and bit down on his fist to stop himself from smashing it against a wall. He shouldn't care about her after everything she'd done but now he worried why she would have stolen from him? The person he knew in Cara would never have done such a thing and he sat up night after night worrying if she might be in some trouble. He wished he could have approached it all differently, maybe given her the chance to explain. Instead he had pushed her away, only managing to punish them both. He felt frustration rise up again within him as he remembered his belongings falling out onto her clothing as she packed to leave. He was a sucker for worrying about her and yet he constantly battled with the evidence in front of him and the person he had grown to know. He should worry about the trouble she was causing him and not these idealised notions of her, he thought as he punched the wall anyways. He needed a distraction, someone to take his mind off Cara. A way for him to release all his pent up irritation and confusion in a more constructive manner.

He picked up his phone and dialled his last fling. Jeri was a little too kinky in the bedroom for his liking but he needed that right now. The last thing he wanted was somebody who wanted him to hold them afterwards. He arranged a date for that coming Friday but already he was having second thoughts, he went to bed deciding he would cancel on Jeri the next day and concentrate on work instead.

***

Cara smiled as she listened to Vanessa and Mae chatter away about their favourite books. They both got on amazingly and it was so uplifting to see Mae happy. Her illness had left her a weak and unable to enjoy life with same zest she'd once possessed and now Cara could see it return. She was gaining strength and even insisted that they start going for short walks as soon as the weather picked up. Cara left them alone as she finished the house work and wondered about maybe taking up busking in the evenings to help with bills over the Christmas period. She was finally beginning to feel better after a bad strain of the common cold and really wanted her and Mae to get back to how it used to be. Jack was always on her mind and she regretted deeply their last argument. She wished she could turn back the clock and erase the whole thing but unfortunately she would have to live with how she reacted to his cruelty. She stood up from polishing the bookshelf and felt a little light headed, she grabbed the shelves holding herself up before moving into the kitchen for a snack. *You need to eat more!* She scolded herself putting away her cleaning equipment and starting lunch.

***

Jack spent the week working from early in the morning until late at night. He checked his phone regularly hoping to hear from Cara but nothing. He hated to admit it to himself but he missed her. The woman knew how to push all his buttons, good and bad. He liked the idea that she was independent but the thoughts of her out in the world with no one to protect her, taking care of her ill aunt and in some kind of financial trouble worried him. He hated the idea of her having to work in dingy clubs or wait tables just to cover Mae's medical bills, but she was too proud to accept his help anymore. His plan had been to see out the full month with Cara and then go their separate ways, he felt robbed of those last few days, as well as everything else. He thought of barely anything else and he knew he needed to move on before he became completely obsessed with her.

The more time she spent apart from Jack the more she seemed to miss him. Mae told her time would heal the pain but her heart break was still a gaping wound. Cara was doing everything to try keep herself busy but she was feeling ill again and spent most of her time stuck indoors taking care of Mae. The unbelievable sense of despair she'd felt when Jack had believed her capable of stealing was the only thing that was beginning to improve. She ran it over again and again in her mind trying to understand how anyone could do such an awful thing and trying to figure out who the culprit could be. David and Jenny seemed too sweet to hide such an evil streak and the only person that made sense in her mind was Julie. Jenny had mentioned that she was annoyed to have been pushed out so that Cara could work for the month. Cara blew out a frustrated breath as she lay on her bed, it was pointless trying to pin-point anyone, she had only met Julie once and again there was no way she would ever dream of making such an accusation. Her mind wandered back to Jack as she turned on her side looking out her bedroom window. It was going to take time to trust herself again where a man was concerned after Jack, everything about him had raised red flags, all of which she'd ignored. It was hard to accept that she needed to take responsibility for her own pain. Rationally she could dissect everything and see things from his point of view. But emotionally she couldn't understand how, after they'd shared so much intimacy, he could throw her out into the cold dark night; without even listening to her or giving her a chance to explain. He made up his mind that she was guilty and it frightened her that she had overlooked that side of his character. Cara groaned as her head began to thump from the stress of rerunning it all again. She wished she could forget him and all that went on but right now it was impossible. Flashes of their shared nights haunted her every time she closed her eyes and it saddened her, to think, that it could have all been an act. She felt he played her and she was the silly fool who jump straight into his arms. She cringed, remembering how easy it had all been for him, how easy she had made it. She twisted again in her bed still looking out her window, there was nothing but another concrete apartment block to look at but it helped her to stare into space. It often lead to daydreams about Jack coming to apologise and beg for her forgiveness, telling her he had nabbed the real villain and that he was sorry he ever doubted her. She picked up her cell phone once more just to double check no one had called before drifting off to sleep.

During the night Cara bolted from her bed to the bathroom, a violent nauseousness succumbed her as she emptied her stomach. She stood splashing her face, got some water and returned to bed rubbing her aching tummy. The last few weeks had been one thing after another and she decided that she would go see the doctor in the morning to try and get to the bottom of why she was so run down.

She woke the next morning still queasy and dragged herself into Mae's room. Mae was sitting up in her bed reading when Cara entered;

"Mae, I'm not well" she moaned clenching her stomach as a new wave of cramping besieged her.

"Cara sit dow…." Mae's words echoed through her mind as the room spun and everything went black.

She woke a few seconds later, her body limp as Mae tried to lift her from the floor.

"Mae no stop" she pushed her weakly away.

"Cara I can't lift you…" Mae was frantic as she continued to try help "…I'll be right back, don't try get up" she rushed as she placed a pillow under Cara's head and left.

Cara felt some strength return "I'm feeling better, don't worry" she whispered her voice as weak as her body. Even in her dizzy mind she worried Mae would hurt herself, trying to help her.

"Ok Dr. Roberts is on the way" Mae bound back into the room carrying water.

"He said to drink some water and not to move."

Cara did as she was told and sipped some of the cold water, her eyelids were too heavy to open and her body ached all over. Her shoulders, back and stomach the worse.

Mae left her a few minutes later to go answer the door and Cara, using the bed as leverage, tried to pull herself from the floor;

"Whoa steady now" she felt strong arms come around her waist and help her fully onto the bed.

"Let's get you lying down" Dr Roberts's calm voice instantly reassured her that she would be ok. She couldn't remember a time when she felt so completely broken.

"Ok let me look you over" he said as he began pushing gently on her stomach.

"She has been ill for a few weeks now" Mae piped in and Cara hated hearing her sound so concerned.

"Tell me if you feel any pain Cara"

"My stomach s and lower back are cramping and my shoulders are paining me" she opened her eyes and tried to make out the blurry images. After blinking a few times everything began to come back into focus.

She could feel some energy return to her body and was now embarrassed for having worried everyone so much.

"Cara when was your last menstrual cycle?" Dr Roberts asked as he took her blood pressure.

She thought for a few minutes, trying to remember "Ummmm I can't be sure doctor, maybe seven weeks ago" she blushed.

"Is there any possibility you could be pregnant?"

"No, not really…. I guess, oh God I don't know. I'm on the pill but I did forget some days" she sat up straight in the bed her eyes finding Mae's.

"Ok I will need to do a urine and blood test to check." Cara looked away as the needle went into her arm, she held her breath when she felt the slight pinch and let it out when Dr Roberts said "All done."

"I will help you to the bathroom and give you some privacy so we can do the urine sample, it will give us a good idea if you are pregnant."

Cara placed the little pot beside the sink as she washed her hands, looking into the mirror she barely recognised the gaunt face before her. No matter what the results she promised herself that she would start looking after her body from today. She looked down at her tummy, rubbing her hand across it, *Jack's baby* she thought as the fear and dread of what could be hit her.

She opened the door to let the doctor in and watched as he dipped little colourful sticks into her urine. He poured the cup down the toilet and opened the bin disposing of it and his gloves before washing his hands and turning to her. The suspense of it all was unbearable "Let's go back inside shall we" he said allowing her to walk ahead, back into Mae's room.

"Would you like to speak in private?" he asked looking to Mae and then to Cara.

"No, I want Mae here."

He smiled fondly to them both and Cara sat on the bed. "Ok Cara my initial findings show that you are indeed pregnant…" he eyed Cara carefully allowing the information to sink in "… however, with the cramping, especially the shoulder pain, I'm worried that you could be about to miscarry" his tone was soft as he broke the news to her.

Cara was a ball of emotions, instantly a need to protect her unborn child had her reaching again for her stomach. Her eyes watered as she tried to digest that in one hand she had been given a child and in the other it might be all taken straight away from her.

"Can I do anything?" she murmured.

"Right now all you can do is stay in bed, no walking around, no cleaning, and no strenuous activity at all."

"What can I do ?" Mae asked, stepping forward and coming to sit by Cara. Cara felt the comfort of Mae's support as her arms tightened around her.

"I think you need to get yourself better Mae, Is there anyone who can help? The Father maybe?" he queried and Cara looked straight to Mae shaking her head no.

"No" Mae said defiantly "we will figure it out."

"Ok well I need to get these bloods to the lab for official confirmation, Cara you need plenty of fluids. You're de-hydrated and have a viral infection, so eat as much as you can and stay off your feet for the foreseeable future."

"Thank you so much for coming" Mae stood to see him out.

"Thank you doctor" Cara finished and she made her way to her bed, climbing in and staying there for the rest of the morning.

Mae fussed about her and later that afternoon Dr Roberts phoned to confirm that the bloods showed she was most definitely pregnant and in fact iron deficient. Mae was insisting that she go to the pharmacy to buy supplies, against Cara's adamant refusals. When the door bell sounded and Ann arrived in with a bag of recommended vitamins and iron the argument ceased.

Cara followed all of the doctors' orders and after three days of bed rest the cramping was finally beginning to ease. Her recent news churned over in her mind and she flitted from moments of joy and excitement to fear and dread. Having a baby on her own was going to be hard work, she had no job and Mae was still quite ill. Every time she thought about telling Jack her stomach cramped a little worse than before and she knew she couldn't face doing it right now. He needed to be told, and she would, without a doubt inform him but right now while her little baby was so fragile inside her, all she could think to do was protect herself and her unborn child.

Mae was her rock, as always, reassuring her that everything was going to work out. A new life, a beautiful little precious gift could never be a bad thing, no matter what the circumstances.

Chapter Eight

Cara was going stir crazy in her bed after a week of bed rest. Vanessa and Ann stopped by almost every day bringing her treats and books to read. Ann was also making sure she was taking her vitamins and was obsessed with checking her blood pressure. It was nice to feel loved and safe. Mae was already getting out the knitting needles and wanted to start a blanket for the baby but until Cara got the all clear she would hold off.

She lay on her bed and knew, today was the day she would tell Jack. She would figure out exactly what she wanted to say and go to him. She was a nervous wreck but he was their baby's Father and he deserved to know. Tonight when he got home from work she would be there.

Jack was typing away at his computer when his phone buzzed.

Hey sexy, you free tonight? x

It was another message from Jeri. He should have known better than to contact her again, she had been trying to get him to reschedule their date ever since he cancelled the week before.

He was about to decline again but had second thoughts. *Do I really want to spend another Friday night alone?* His apartment used to be his sanctuary but now everywhere he looked, all he could see was Cara. Cara in his

bed, Cara in his kitchen, Cara in his study ….. He needed to remember how good it felt to be young free and
single *and quite good looking* be scoffed. She might not
want anything to do with him anymore but Jeri did, she
was texting him, she thought about him, why should he
continue to pine after someone who hated his guts?
He needed to try to move on and get back to his old life,
when not caring, actually meant not caring. He made the
decision the week before to hire a private detective. He
knew everything pointed to Cara but something was
telling him, that he may have been wrong. His gut never
stirred him wrong and when he finally realised that it
wasn't just wishful thinking that she could be innocent
but more a deep rooted belief in her, he made the decision to get to the bottom of it. He thought about phoning
her and asking her to meet him, to explain if she was in
some kind of trouble, but his pride stopped him every
time. If she did do it, he knew it was drastic measure on
her part and he longed to find out why and to help. Surely it should be her to come to him? His mind boggled
once again as he got wrapped up in the, he said, she said
of it all. He ran his hands through his thick hair as he
remembered their last encounter, she despised him. Jack
slammed his fist down on the desk and picked up his
phone, he would call Jeri and begin to move on with his
life. There was too much water under the bridge with
Cara, too many things had been said and done for either
of them to forgive.

Cara arrived at Jacks that evening. Mae was upset at her for going out into the cold but she needed to do it now or she feared she never would. She hailed a taxi cab there and would get one home, she would stay off her feet as much as she could, it was now or never. She feared that telling Jack about the baby would mean him accusing her of trying to trap him. She pulled her dark blue over-coat tightly around her body as she stepped from the cab, despite her pink hat and scarf the cold wind cut through her. She walked into the foyer and pressed the call button for his condo. When there was no answer she decided to wait outside for him to return. He might be angry if she was indoors. It didn't matter either way she supposed, he would probably always think the worse of her. She crossed the street and waited under the shelter of a different apartment block. She looked at her watch, it was 7.30p.m, her tummy did somersaults knowing he would be home soon.

She looked around the pristine neighbourhood as she waited, admiring the Christmas lights that twinkled from the garlands that lined the buildings. Vanessa and Ann promised to help get them a tree and both her and Mae were excited to get Christmas started. It was only a week away, normally they would have it done in early December but this year was different. She rubbed her belly again, her little baby would be here next year and everything would be so much more magical. She would have loved to have her Mom and Dad around to meet their grandchild and hoped that Jack would at least want to get to know his child. Her Dad treated her like his little princess and she wanted nothing less for her own child. Her eyes watered again, remembering some of her earlier Christmases, before her world was torn apart and she made her own Christmas wish now. Her hormones were wreaking havoc with her emotions and she found herself crying at the drop of a hat. She thought back to when Jack had broken her heart that first night and wondered if that pain was part of those changing hormones *no just plain old heart break* she conceded as she looked back onto the street as Jacks black Mercedes pulled up.

Jack skipped starters and dessert; he made yet another mistake by coming here. He was more interested in a life of celibacy, than he was in dating Jeri. Everything she said and did grated on him and although she was a beautiful woman, she wasn't Cara. He was a fool for believing that he could forget Cara by sleeping with Jeri. It was the opposite, every feline purr and eye lash bat that she faked only reaffirmed for him that Cara was the person he wanted to be with. He had spent his life avoiding these feelings, hiding behind the rich bachelor façade to keep women at a distance, until Cara. She was everything he never knew he wanted. She was real. She looked at him with genuine feelings whether it was lust, anger, *love!* He held his chest at his last thought, did she love him? Did he love her? Looking at Jeri now the idea of sleeping with her, only made him want Cara more. He felt the old familiar walls come up at the idea of giving that side of himself to anyone. He needed to get away from Jeri, away from New York and try to figure out what he wanted.

"Are we going back to yours?" Jeri broke through his thoughts as she slid across the leather car seat whispering in his ear. Her seduction methods had once thrilled him and now they seemed lacking. Cara never tried to look or be sexy around him and yet she was the sexiest woman he ever met.

"I just need to grab one or two things and I will drop you home straight away" he turned away looking out the window. It was cruel he knew, but tonight was the last time he and Jeri would be in each other's company. He was going to grab a few things and go stay at his home in Hudson Valley. Could he forgive Cara and try again? Would she want to? Was he willing to risk his pride and look a fool? All these questions spun around his head along with the images of their time together, her face, her laugh, her naked flesh against his.

"Oh I see you are excited to get me home" Jeri purred as she ran her hand along the inside of his leg. Jack grabbed her hand before it reached its destination.

"Not tonight Jeri" his tone was cold and flat but it was time to let Jeri know he was done.

"This is it for us, no more dates or sleep overs" he watched as her eyes narrowed and her flesh reddened with rage from the rejection. Jeri was not the kind of woman to get upset over a man, yes the rejection would sting for a day or two but she would soon move on to her next prey.

He watched her compose herself as best she could, as they pulled up at his condo. Jack was directing Lucas to take Jeri home when she interrupted;

"No, If it is okay with you, I need to use the ladies room" she smiled sweetly.

Jack rolled his eyes and held the door open for her as she stuck her long legs out of the car, the toes of her black stilettos pointing up, she yet again tried to use her body to seduce him. As she stepped into the cold night she snuggled into her fur jacket and moved closer to Jack "Just one last time" she pouted like a child, before walking ahead of him giggling like a naughty school girl. Jack followed behind, determined to get her in and out as soon as possible. He didn't have time for her games, his decision was made and unlike before he would not be seeking her out again. *Cara has lot to answer for*, he thought, leaving Julie in charge of Jeri and making his way into his room to pack a bag. He was no longer able to enjoy a woman's company without wishing she was Cara, even the female form wasn't enough to tempt him even when it was offered up free and on a plate. He only wanted Cara.

Cara watched as all her mini daydreams of that afternoon disappeared into the cold night air. She seen Jack's car and was walking towards him; when she noticed a beautiful woman step out of the car and rub herself all over him in the middle of the street. The woman looked familiar as Cara squinted to see her face, from a distance it looked like the same woman he had been with in Hudson Valley. *Was Jack seeing this woman all along?* It seemed impossible; they spent almost every night together while she was here. *No, she was just another one of his flings before he returned to this siren* she realised. Her heart sank as she watched him follow her inside. He was moving on already and she knew she'd been right all along, Jack had just used her. She felt nauseous as she watched this woman rub herself against him, the man she was in love with, the man who was the Father of her baby. Her feet rooted to the spot, she listened to the cackling sounds the woman made, obviously excited for the night ahead. Her throat was raw as unshed tears and emotion fought to the surface. She watched him, type in the key code and climb onto the lift before vanishing to his bed. A deep sense of dread pooled in her stomach, her mind filled with images of them; his arms around her, his mouth on her, their lovemaking, her long nails scratching his back, it was just too much, she had to turn and run. She ran for one block before she remembered the baby and stopped. She wanted to scream, to hit something anything not to feel the unbearable pain that attacked her. *How could he*? She sobbed into her hand as she hailed a taxi. She wanted to go home, to talk to Mae, to be angry and sad and then to go to bed and be alone. It would be a long night imagining everything that they would be doing together, torturing herself with her own memories of their love making and hoping with her, he would be different. She couldn't believe that she'd been just another notch in his belt; she needed to stop believing in him.

***

Cara sat up straight breathing hard as she woke from her sleep. The pain in her chest from last night remained, and she broke down again. She wished this feeling would go, that the physical pain of her heart break would pass soon. She could handle the emotional trauma, if everything else left her. This grief was so deep and raw she wondered if it ever went away. She tried breathing easier in the hope her constricted chest would become lighter but no calming mediation took away the ache, it lived there, for now. Mae promised her it would get better but only time would tell, she couldn't see how. Her stomach rumbled and she considered staying in bed for the day, but remembered her baby. She lay back on the pillow and allowed herself to cry, she would not bottle up her pain, she would release it so she could be free from it. She rolled onto her back and began to feel her stomach, her body hadn't changed yet but Cara could already feel love for her unborn baby. She cried a little as the realisation that, not only time, but also her baby would help to heal her heart. She could choose to spend her time crying or she could get her head together and make plans for their future. She wiped her eyes and picked up one of the pregnancy books, Vanessa had brought her. There was seven months to prepare for her new baby but her role as a Mammy started today.

Your midwife may need to snip the perineum to help get the baby out … "Eeeewwwww" Cara slammed the book closed over an hour later. She may have been a little too curious when she skipped straight to the Giving Birth section. She listened as Mae put on some Christmas music and decided to join her in the living room. She was strictly still on bed rest so she would need to take it easy today, especially after yesterday's upset. She came out still dressed in her pyjamas and her red house coat to find Mae decorating the tree. She smiled from the doorway as she watched Mae; she was almost back to her full self. Mae's enthusiasm for the baby helped her accept it and even become excited herself. Moments like these reminded Cara that there was a life before Jack Copper and there will be life after him. "Sleigh bells ring are you listening…" she began to join in with the cd, hugging Mae before relaxing and singing from the couch, the lights twinkled and the tinsel glistened on the tree. It was beginning to feel like Christmas.

***

The hallways of Hudson Valley were haunted with memories of Cara. He walked to his quarters and swore he could almost hear her husky voice echo throughout the large mansion. This was his fourth night here and he only felt further from Cara. He missed her, and this feeling wasn't going anywhere soon. Stripping from his suit Jack entered the walk-in shower; water cascaded down his hard body as he tried to wash away the stress. He longed to forget her touch, it had changed his life and no matter how hard he fought, it stayed with him. Every inch of him had been claimed by her and his heart followed suit. He never stood a chance; he could see that now remembering the first moment he set eyes on her. She was like a beacon of light that called to him as she ran towards the hospital, her golden hair intruding on what would have been a bleak grey day. The moment he looked into her big blue eyes, he knew then, like he knew now, he wanted her. He fought her every step of the way, afraid to give that last piece of himself to her, his heart. Love destroyed his family and he thought he could avoid it. He thought coming here would help him move on; instead he was pulled back to his childhood. His Grandfather raised him in this house and it was a lonely childhood. Jack would never forget the night his parents died, he was six. He sat with his Grandfather in the hospital waiting room. They told him his Father was dead and they waited for hours, hoping his Mother would make it. They had been in a car crash, he sat silent as his Grandfather prayed that his daughter would pull through. The moment the doctor spoke the dreaded words "she's gone" everything changed for them both. They left the hospital different people; his Grandfather became cold and distant. He lost his only child that night, the apple of his eye and he was unable to love Jack. Jack never wanted for anything, except love. His life may have been empty of emotion but Cara managed to rekindle something within him and he wanted to be better for her. He wanted to give her all of him, to step into unknown territory and open his heart. He would swallow his pride and put his faith in her. If she was in trouble he would fix it, no matter what it cost. He towelled himself and dressed quickly, he needed to get back to the city. If he was going to win her back he would need to put a plan in place.

Chapter

Nine

Two days later Jack climbed the steps of Cara's brown-stone apartment. It was Christmas Eve and almost four weeks since he last seen Cara. He listened at the door as she sang Christmas carols with Mae, she sounded happy. He looked down at his outfit not sure if he made the right decision, he'd settled on dark jeans, a burgundy shawl neck jumper and a grey duffle coat. He braced himself once more before knocking; if she was happy without him he would accept it.

If she didn't need him, like he needed her then he would walk away with his head held high and never bother her again. Rejection was likely after how he had treated her but she was worth risking his pride for. He pressed the doorbell and waited for her to answer.

Cara laughed from the couch. She practically lived in this spot and it was officially her corner now. Mae was sipping over a glass of wine as they both sang *Rudolf the red nose reindeer.* Christmas Eve was a bitter sweet time for her, as a child she missed out on too many Christmases with her parents but she also cherished the memories of the ones they shared together. Mae always made an extra special effort this time of year and Cara never doubted that she was loved. Mae had made her the woman she was today and she would always be thankful for her. They had everything ready for Christmas Day, the gifts were wrapped under the tree and the turkey was cooking in the oven. They planned to watch a movie and un-wrap one gift before bed. The door bell sounded and

Mae dragged herself up from under their fluffy blanket to answer it.

"Who could that be?"

"Maybe the neighbours to complain about our singing" Cara giggled hiding her face under the blanket "I'm not here" she laughed as Mae opened the door.

"Ah-hem" Cara peeked out from the blanket as Mae cleared her throat. The atmosphere changed in an instant from fun to grim when her eyes met with a very coy looking Jack Cooper. His large frame made their small living room seem tiny as he stared at her, saying nothing. He looked different, softer and his eyes lacked their usual angry glint. Her stomach turned as he held her captivated, just looking at him fanned the flames of her smouldering attraction towards him. She realised she looked a mess and she fixed her mussed hair behind her ears.

"Coffee?" Mae broke the painful silence. Jack turned to Mae, breaking eye contact and giving her a chance to breathe easy.

"Mae, you look really well."

"Thank you, Jack." Mae smiled warmly at him, despite everything that happened between Cara and Jack, he had saved Mae's life and they both would always feel indebted to him.

"I'm sorry to interrupt your Christmas Eve but would it be okay if I have a few moments alone with Cara?" he turned to Cara "If that's ok with you?" he asked.

This is new Cara thought, he normally demanded she speak with him. Cara nodded to Mae, whatever his reason for coming she wanted it to be over with as soon as possible.

"Yes I still have some wrapping to do" Mae lied as she kissed Cara's cheek and moved swiftly to her bedroom. Cara pulled her body up and hugged her knees. Her legs still wrapped in the warm fleece blanket.

"Why are you here Jack?"

"Is it ok if I sit?" he looked nervous and Cara wondered what would cause him to act so out of character.

"I have a Christmas gift for you" he reached into his pocket and handed Cara an envelope. She held it in her hands for a few moments not sure what to do with it.

"Why have you brought me a present?"

"It's Christmas, and at Christmas you give the people you care about a gift" he shrugged. It was such a simple and honest response, it left her speechless. She turned it over in her hand.

"But... I don't understand" she whispered her hand trembling slightly as she opened the sealed envelope. She looked up at him once more; the tension was palpable between them. He was watching her as the lights from the Christmas tree flicked from blue, to green and red, the colours reflecting on his face. She pulled a leaflet from the envelope and read the contents; "Switzerland?!" she said out loud, in shock at the extravagant gift.

"You deserve to be whisked away and spoiled for a few days" he announced ruefully.

"I ... I ... But why?"

Her mind boggled as she tried to figure out what he was trying to say. *Had his last affair ended and he needed another replacement?* The remembered pain of seeing him with another woman shook her from the magical moment. This was all very over the top but she wasn't looking to be his live in lover anymore. She deserved more, their child deserved more and she would rather be alone than settle for less than one hundred percent.

"I can't go… thanks….but I'm sure you will find someone else" She reached forward handing him back the envelope "Take it" she demanded when he just sat there looking at it.

"It's for you Cara, no one else."

"But I don't want it Jack, you can't just come here without warning, hand me a gift without an explanation and expect me to just take it" she moved her body back further from him until she hit he arm of the couch. Jack reached forward to take the envelope, his fingers caressing hers and taking her hand instead. She tried to tug it free but he only tightened his grip.

"Cara I'm sorry for how I treated you, I miss you, I don't care about everything that has happened, I would like us to start over" his thumb caressed her palm as he spoke his eyes never leaving hers.

"Did you miss me the whole time Jack?" her cold tone causing his brow to furrow.

"Yes" he answered warily.

"Did you miss me last Friday night Jack?" Cara pulled her hand free from his "because I sat for hours outside your apartment waiting for you to come home" she continued.

Jack searched his mind back to the previous Friday and the realisation that Cara had seen him with Jeri finally dawned on him.

"Cara it's not what you think I promise" he panicked. He hadn't anticipated this and was like a deer in headlights as he tried to figure a way to explain it.

"It was exactly what I think Jack, please don't insult me by denying it" she folded her arms across her chest and turned her face away from him. She didn't want to hear him explain away his latest fling, it was none of her business really but she would not be his fall back lover. She loved him and anything less than that wasn't good enough for her. Her eyes watered as she tried to swallow the lump in her throat. She didn't want to think of seeing him with her and remember every image of them together that she had conjured up in her mind.

"Cara..." his voice was soft as he turned her face to look at him "Jeri was an old fling, who I used to distract me from you. I didn't sleep with her, she left soon after I arrived home."

She tried to shake his hand from her face so she could look away again but his gentle strength held her in place, forcing her to look into his eyes.

"I wanted only you then, and now. I promise you I will never hurt you again."

A few stray tears escaped and he quickly wiped them from her face.

"I saw you both together, I thought you had moved on" Cara sniffed.

"You're not that easy to get over Cara. I thought I could if I met Jeri but all it did was reconfirm that it is you I want. Nobody else" his thumb ran along her bottom lip as he moved closer.

She felt his breath on her face before she pulled away "I can't Jack" she whispered her voice betraying her. She sounded weak and that's how she felt because despite everything she still loved him; still wanted him.

"You hurt me, you accused me of stealing and said some horrible things" her wounded pride needed to confront him before she could forgive it.

"I can see I've hurt you Cara, I'm so sorry" he kissed her cheek and stood to leave. She watched amazed as he prepared to walk away from her again and her heart called after him.

He couldn't sit here any longer and upset her. She deserved a nice Christmas and he was only hurting her further. Turning from her was like walking on hot coal as he willed his body to keep moving.

"Jack" the sweet sound of his name on her lips gave him hope as he turned back to face her. She looked small and fragile amongst the oversized blanket that covered her.

"I can't just be somebody's lover, if that's what you came here for…."

"It's not…" he interrupted her smiling from ear to ear. This was his chance right here and it felt so good to have one. "…I want to go away with you and spend time together, get to know each other... as my girlfriend" he shrugged a little embarrassed, he hadn't had a girlfriend since high school.

"Oh"

"I know it's a lot to ask but I really want to try make this work."

Cara nodded at him smiling her eyes watery again. He came to her now taking her face in his hands and kissed her gently on the lips, just one soft kiss to seal the deal. His forehead rested against hers for a moment before he kissed her again.

He sat back looking at her now and noticed for the first time that she looked pale.

"Are you ok?" he asked, suddenly concerned for her health.

He watched her fidget slightly before looking away "I just have some stomach pains" she lied to him.

She was a terrible liar and he wondered what she was hiding. He realised that this was the first time she had ever lied to him. His instinct that she was telling the truth about the missing jewellery was confirmed in that moment. He decided to let it go, for now, whatever was wrong with her was her own business unless it worsened. In the meantime this was his opportunity to take care of her, and he was not about to pass it up.

Cara landed herself in hot water, she wanted to tell Jack about the baby but she froze. It was the perfect opportunity but selfishly she wanted him to herself for now. She didn't know how he might take the news that he was going to be a Father, he could ask her to terminate or even accuse her of trapping him.

He was making an effort with her but how would the news of the baby effect his decision? What if he changed his mind about her again in a day or two? She needed a few days with him to figure out if he meant all the things he said tonight. If he stayed, she would hope he might be happy and if he left then she hoped he would still be a part of his child's life. Either way she would tell him after Christmas.

"So did you miss me?"

"Nope" she giggled playfully as he pulled her onto his lap.

"Oh really? Well I missed you like a hole in the head" he shot back before kissing her long and hard.

She pulled back breathless from his kiss "well…maybe a little" she teased before kissing him right back.

They settled on the couch talking about their time apart, neither mentioning the missing jewellery. Cara wasn't ready for that fallout again but she hoped he might start to believe her. If they stood any chance of being together they needed to trust one another. *What about Jeri, do I believe him?* Her own doubts crept in. She pushed them aside for now, they could figure all that out later, right now she was too happy to ruin it.

"I can't wait to take you to Switzerland" he whispered against her neck.

"When I'm feeling better I think it will be fabulous... *especially with a crying baby"* she kept the last thought to herself. Jack stood from the chair and lifted her in his arms;

"Let's get you to bed"

"Jack, I can't, we can't... Not tonight." she mumbled into his chest, the familiar scent sending waves of desire coursing through her body. She burned for his touch and wanted nothing more than to make love to him but she wanted to take things slow this time. It was a curse being so attracted to the man; he tested her will power with just his smell. She could be blind and his spicy aroma would leave her begging for him.

He lay her down on her bed and propped up her pillows; "I want to be with you anyway I can tonight and I'll wait until you can trust me again before we go any further" he leaned down kissing her before removing his shoes and lying beside her.

Cara groaned into her pillow at his caring gesture, it was going to be a long night. Already her fingers tingled to touch him and he was fully clothed. She knew it was safe to have sex with him, the doctor had reassured her that everything seemed ok but advised she take it easy as much as she could. They both lay sideways on top of the duvet facing each other. Her red fleece blanket was too big for one person and she spread it across covering his body. They both smiled like teenagers as they kissed and cuddled in their makeshift cocoon.

"It's nice just spending time together."

"You look so pretty" he beamed at her.

"Yea kind of like Cinderella before all the magic, this is the stuff fairy tales right here" she pointed to her frizzy hair and pale face. He began to laugh at her silly joke and she joined in, she had never seen him look so young and carefree before. It made her happy to see him so relaxed with her.

"Can I ask you something?"

"Yes"

"Will you tell me about your childhood?" she knew he hated talking about himself but she really wanted to know everything about him.

"There isn't much to tell Cara, my parents died when I was young and my Grandfather brought me up" he leaned forward kissing her softly.

"Do you miss them?" she whispered against his lips as he tried to silence her.

"Every day, but the pain has lessened over the years."

"Jack, I'm sorry". She herself knew about loss and she reached over running her fingers lightly across his forehead, un-furrowing his eyebrows. She didn't want to upset him or make him uncomfortable and she was surprised when he continued on with the story.

"My Mother was a nurse and my father was a doctor. They both met when he treated her in his E.R late one night. She came in with appendicitis and he was her doctor. They both grew up four blocks from each other, and worked in different departments of the same hospital for three years before they met" Jack smiled and Cara reached for his hand encouraging him to continue. "The usual story my Dad fell madly in love and vice versa they married quickly and had me not too long after that. I remember the night they died; they had left me with my Grandfather to attend a function at the hospital. My Dad had two drinks and lost control of the car."

Cara snuggled closer to him, kissing him deeply. She wanted to take away the pain but knew it was not something you could wipe away. Losing your parents at a young age was crippling in so many ways, and they both shared this awful experience.

"I'm sorry" she leaned back again looking into his sorrowful eyes.

"It took me a long time to forgive my Father. My Grandfather died resenting him and me for being his son. I found my Mothers diary when I was in my early twenties, she catalogued their love story and I read how much he loved her. He was a good husband and loved her deeply, she knew it and in the end one reckless act took them from me, I decided it was time to let go and forgive him."

Jack wrapped his arms around Cara and wondered if this was how his Father felt when he held his Mother. The world was starting to make sense and he was finally allowing himself to be, for, and because of her. He kissed her again they stayed like this all night, talking and sharing, kissing and snuggling, until they both fell asleep in the early hours.

***

She could feel his lips on her neck as he nudged her awake "Happy Christmas" he whispered in her ear trying to seduce her into waking up. Cara stretched her arms and smiled as he continued to kiss along her collar bone, before she opened her eyes. His warm body left hers and she pouted missing his mouth on her.

"I'll be back in a minute, open your eyes I left a gift for you" he said as he left. Cara sat up straight away and smiled at the small gift wrapped box and folded piece of paper on the opposite pillow waiting for her. She was giddy as she grabbed it and began reading;

Happy Christmas Cara
This is your first gift today..
I hope you like it
Jack xx

She tore open the gift wrap to reveal a black necklace box. With unsteady hands she lifted the lid to find a beautiful gold locket sitting on a red velvet cushion. Removing it gently from the box, she turned it in her hand and was reading the inscription when Jack walked in carrying breakfast on a tray.

She looked up at him;

"It's beautiful" she kneeled before him kissing him on the lips before looking down at the locket again.

"*Forever in my heart*"

"Open it" he urged and she looked inside the little gold heart. Two small pictures of her parents sat on either side and she gasped in amazement at such a thoughtful gift.

"Jack, it's so…" words couldn't describe how touched she was. He settled the tray on the bedside locker before joining her on the bed and planting a chaste kiss on her lips.

"Happy Christmas, I hope you like it."

He smelt like cinnamon and coffee and she wanted to taste him again.

"I love it…" she grabbed him deepening the kiss.

"Where did you get the photos?" she wondered a few minutes later as they ate breakfast in bed.

"Mae helped me with them this morning."

"It's the most thoughtful gift anyone has ever given me Jack, I will cherish it forever" she promised.

He moved the empty tray from her lap and settled her on his, as he kissed her again. She moved to pull away a few minutes later but Jack's hand moved up and slid behind her neck holding her in place. She could feel his arousal beneath her and felt her own body respond to his kiss. She pulled away once more and looked into his dark green eyes, their noses still touching. His hand was still tangled up in her hair and her breath was still a little jagged.

"I'm afraid you're going to hurt me" she admitted to him. He was being everything she hoped for and more and her heart couldn't take another rejection from him.

"I promise you I'm not going anywhere."

"Okay" she smiled weakly.

"I'll leave you to get dressed and then we can open more gifts" he said and stood from the bed, smiling as he exited the room. Cara was still looking at the door when he walked straight back in.

"I realise that I said I wasn't going anywhere and then I left! But I'm just in the other room."

Cara giggled at him as he tried to reassure her. He was so cute sometimes.

***

Jack spent Christmas morning with her and Mae. He was attentive and loving, making sure she was comfortable on the couch while he helped Mae in the kitchen. When Mae eventually shooed him out from under her feet he joined Cara on the sofa, settling her between his legs as he kissed and massaged her shoulders.

"Time for your second gift" he announced a little while later as he jumped up retrieving a second envelope from his jacket.

"I can't take another gift, I haven't given you anything."
"This is a gift for me too" he winked.

Cara looked over the envelope, *there was no way he managed to cram sexy lingerie in there* she thought as she tried to imagine what it could possibly be. She slid a finger under the crease, ripping it open and reading the contents.

"JACK!!" she squealed "You're crazy, you're having a recording studio built??" her mouth was wide open as she clutched the letter, reading it again.

To: Jack Cooper C.E.O

From: Lucy Wilkes, Property Solutions

Dear Mr Cooper,

This email is to confirm the commencement of work on a home studio at your Hudson Valley estate.

Isabelle our interior designer will be on site January 5th at 11am.

"Well I'm having some rooms converted, I can build you one in New York if you prefer?" Cara looked up at him in awe, he meant every word, he would do that for her, if she asked.

"This is too much Jack…"

"It's not, I want you to have everything you deserve, plus, like I said, it's for me too."

"How?" she laughed grabbing a tissue, wiping her eyes.

"I want the first cd for my car"

"I can't believe, I'll get to record my own songs!"

"Yes, I can get you an agent if you like?"

Shaking her head she leaned over and kissed him on the couch "No, I don't want to be famous, I just want to sing" she smiled lovingly into his green eyes.

Jack gripped her around the waist and hugged her against his hard chest.

"I don't have any gift for you" she wished now that she had bought him something, just in case.

"I already got my Christmas wish" his finger trailed down her moist cheek as she looked up from his chest.

Bending his head he seized her lips with his.

"I better stop before I lose control" he groaned, pulling away from her.

"I want you so bad" she murmured against his lips and hated herself for denying them both what they needed, the night before.

"You do huh?" his eyes narrowed as he tugged her bottom lip with his teeth, causing heat to pool in her stomach.

"Sorry to break up the love fest, but dinner is ready." Cara and Jack jumped back like bold children when Mae walked in. Taking her hand, he helped her from the couch as they joined Mae at the dining table.

***

Sitting back on the couch again Cara felt guilty as Mae and Jack cleaned up after dinner. She wanted to help but they both insisted she relax. Jack tried to get Mae to join her while he did everything but Mae refused to hear of it. Cara folded her arms on the back of the sofa, resting her chin on them and she looked on into the kitchen. Her eyes travelled up and down Jacks body *beaut* she thought as his strong sexy back flexed.

She thought about their baby that was growing inside of her and hoped that if it was a boy, he would grow up to be like Jack. Yes, he could be grumpy and even aloof but his heart was good. He showed her time and time again just how good he was, from helping Mae to her wonderful gifts. He was thoughtful and caring, a protector. He made her feel safe in his arms and she never wanted to be without him again. No matter how he took the baby news, she would need to be around him for at least the next twenty one years. She hoped they would be together. The secret she was keeping from him now felt like a betrayal, she would tell him when they were alone again. He deserved to know now, before he invested further in their relationship. The door bell sounded and she looked up from her perusal of Jacks fine ass, his eyes glinting as he turned catching her.

"That must be your final gift" he smiled rushing to the door.

Cara stood up and walked over to meet him, her eyes knitted together as he spoke with someone at the door. She stood aside as he wheeled in a bright yellow bicycle. It had a white leather seat and a wicker basket sitting on the front. Jack chimed the small silver bell as he held it before her. She covered her mouth and nose with both hands, awed at the beautiful vintage bike. It was the cutest bike she ever laid eyes on and exactly what she would have selected for herself.

The house phone shrilled in the back ground slicing through the silence as Cara circled her new bike.

"I'll get it" Mae smiled as she rubbed Cara's arms smiling at her "I'm so happy for you sweetheart, you deserve this happiness" she reassured her before leaving to get the phone.

Jack propped the bike against the wall, standing back from it nervously;

"If you don't like it, I can take it back. I was going to get you a car but I thought this suited you better" he rambled as she moved to examine the bike. She couldn't speak right now; her words would be lost in a torrent of emotion. She caressed the saddle and crossbar falling in love with it but even more in love with Jack.

"I love it! I love you" she turned unable to hold her feelings in any longer. She was madly, deeply in love with this man who encouraged her to be herself in every way. The pain of the past melted away as she flung her arms around his neck kissing him tenderly, not giving him a chance to say anything. She didn't want to hear him say he didn't feel the same or that it was too soon to say it. She just wanted him to know how he affected her.

Mae came back into the room "Sorry to interrupt… AGAIN" she laughed as she pulled on her jacket "…but that was Vanessa she is coming to pick me up, for the night."

"You don't have to leave" Cara stood back, embarrassed to be running Mae out on Christmas Day.

"We will tone down the mushy stuff" she promised.

"Don't be silly, Vanessa is on her own, you two have fun" she kissed Cara's cheek and looked out the window "There she is" she chirped and collected her overnight bag from the sofa.

"Nice job" she patted Jack's arm as she passed him.

"Happy Christmas" she reached up kissing his cheek before leaving them both alone for the night.

Jack watched as Cara ran back to her bike "I want to sit on it" she said lifting it from the wall, throwing her legs over and balancing herself on the white saddle. She was adorable on it, her red dress hiked up revealing her creamy thigh to him. Her wild hair fell around her face as she bent to look inside the basket;

"What's this?" she pulled out a silver heart shaped key ring from inside.

"Oh I just seen that, I thought you might like it" he blushed as she held it up smiling from ear to ear at the pretty little gift. He was sitting on the arm of the couch as she climbed off the bike and walked to him. She nudged his legs open as she stood between them. Kissing him she softly, she pushed him back onto the couch as she followed him down. He was trapped beneath her and the sofa as her lips moved to his jaw, his neck. The friction of his stubble tingling her soft lips as she moved around tasting every inch of his neck, before nibbling on his earlobe.

Jack flung his legs around, sitting up taking Cara with him, she continued to kiss him, capturing his lips as he carried her to the bedroom. He hoped she wouldn't try stop, he wasn't sure he would be able to. He had been teetering on the edge of madness the past twenty four hours, trying to keep his hands from mauling her beautiful body.

She slid down his body her red dress bunching around her ass, his hands sliding under it as he continued to remove it completely from her body. His fingers gently trailed up and down her arms as he kissed her neck returning her earlier ministrations. She felt his fingers slide under the straps of her bra, moving down her collar bone and delving a little under the cup and back up again. He felt her quiver at his touch as his lips lowered again moving across her breast bone. Her breathing became ragged as he moved the straps down her arms encasing them at her side. His mouth roamed lower as he scooped her breast into his hands, they instantly hardened for him, making his own arousal twitch. His tongue circled her nipples before he sucked gently.

"Jack, I can't" she pushed her hands into his hair pulling him tighter against her breast.

"I want to watch you come for me" his tone was thick with lust as he captured her mouth again, ravishing it.

"Turn around" he whispered. He kissed her shoulders as she turned slowly, moving her hair over the other shoulder. He trailed a line of kisses down her back, undoing her bra clasp as it fell to the floor. He reached her butt gently biting each cheek. She fell back against him as her knees buckled, he stood, moving his hands up her stomach, finding her nipples and squeezing. Her sweet ass was pressed against his stiff manhood as she moved her head to one side giving him full access to her neck. He smiled into her shoulder, delighted at her response.

"Jack" she moaned pulling away, her creamy skin pink from where he had trailed kisses. He was busting out of his jeans just looking at her flushed cheeks, her eyes hungry for him.

He walked her to the edge of the bed and watched her fall back. Removing his jumper and shirt he bent kissing her hard, his fingers sliding under her panties and between her legs, rubbing her sex as he made his way down her body, pulling her underwear away as he went. She was completely naked and his for the taking, he moved lower tasting every inch of her. His tongue stroked her, his fingers moving slowly in and out of her heat. She was wet and ready for him, he devoured her further, as her walls contacted around his fingers and her body shook.

The first wave of pleasure rocked her body at he ceaselessly consumed her. Fire coursed through her, she needed to have him inside her; she sat up as he moved to find her mouth again. She pulled him towards her kissing him urgently and rubbing his erections through his jeans. "Jack I need you inside me, please."

She refused to wait any longer for him as she pulled quickly at his jeans, pulling them of in a heated frenzy. He helped her remove the last of his clothing as he pushed her back on the bed again, kissing her ferociously. He spread her legs with his and settled himself at her entrance; he brushed her hair from her eyes as he pushed into her moistness. Her legs slid up his, as he pumped hard, meeting every unsaid internal need. They kissed and moved to the same rhythm until they both climaxed together.

***

Jack's phone vibrated on the bedside locker waking him from his peaceful sleep. Cara was asleep on one arm as he reach across with the other to pick up the call.

"Jack Cooper" he snapped, at whoever was calling this early, the day after Christmas.

"Hi Jack, it's Dan Fields"

Jack sat up, easing Cara off his arm slowly. Dan was the private detective he hired.

"Dan, what can I do for you?"

"I wondered if we could meet at your office today, I have some things you might find interesting."

Jack looked again at Cara; he knew without a doubt and without proof that she was innocent. He was annoyed now on her behalf and wanted to find the person who tried to hurt her.

"Did you find out who was stealing?"

"Not definitely but I suspect something is amiss. Can we meet at your office today at 2pm? I need to ask you a few more questions to confirm my suspicions."

"Yes, I will see you there" he confirmed, before hanging up.

Jack turned on the phones camera feature and snapped Cara as she slept. He wanted to remember her, just as she looked now.

Jack coming back into her life left Cara walking on air. They made love again that morning before cooking breakfast together. Her cramping had stopped and she was full of energy. Her baby was going to be okay, *their* baby was going to be okay. She was ready to tell Jack today and her initial fear at his reaction now turned to excitement as she longed to share their happy news with him. He knew she loved him, and although he hadn't repeated it, she hoped that he loved her. There was less than seven months to figure it all out and she didn't want to waste another moment. She would shower and do her hair and make-up to help her feel more confident and then she would tell him, no more delays. She chose a plain black dress, with black tights and black ankle boots to wear. She wanted to look good for him and she hoped she was the kind of woman he would be proud to have on his arm. He came in as she finished her mascara and wrapped his arms around her waist kissing her cheek;

"You smell good."

Cara turned in his arms "thanks" she smiled "I thought we could go for a walk?"

"I can't, I need to go into the office for a few hours."

"Oh".

"You look beautiful" he growled into her ear playfully, making her giggle.

"So no chance of me keeping you here for one more day?" she pouted.

"I'll only be one hour; I could go home first, change and then come here after work?"

"Ok great, can we go out for dinner?"

"I'll make reservations and we can go back to mine after dinner for some wine?" he suggested.

Cara stepped out of his embrace and sat at the edge of her bed. She twisted her hands on her lap as she looked up at him, she couldn't lie again "I'm pregnant" she blurted out. He stared expressionless at her, like he had just been punched in the gut and her own stomach turned with nerves. He looked away running his hands through his hair "You're pregnant? *PREGNANT!*" he exclaimed, holding his head. He was dumbfounded and Cara nodded her head confirming it was true "I'm sorry I should have told you yesterday but, I, I didn't know how you would take it" she bit on her bottom lip as he paced her small bedroom. He wasn't angry, which was good but he was still in shock.

"Is it mine?" he stopped suddenly, turning to face her. She flinched at his words "of course, how can you ask me that" her voice was laced with hurt as she looked down at her hands.

"I'm sorry that was uncalled for…but you're pregnant? …I mean, are you sure?" Jack hunched down in front of her. "Look at me" he pleaded with her.

She met his gaze "I'm sorry I asked that" he said kissing her hands.

"I came to tell you last week, when you were with her" Cara stood up from the bed, annoyed that he was questioning her. She wanted to tell him sooner, but Jack was busy with another woman.

"Why didn't you call? How long have you known?" his eyes narrowed down at her.

"Two weeks" she shrugged, not caring if he was angry, she was angry too.

"I didn't tell you because I thought I was losing the baby and I was afraid" she confessed "but when I felt a little better I sought you out straight away, did you want me to interrupt your date?" she snapped.

"I told you that was nothing, don't change the subject! Is this why you have been ill?" his brows quirked.

"Yes, I was on bed rest, but the cramping has stopped!"

"The sex, did I hurt you?" his eyes were wide now as his hands hid his mouth. He looked like he was about to be sick. Cara's stomach churned, this wasn't going good.

"No, I'm fine now" she softened, too tired to fight for him again.

"Cara I don't know what to say, this is all a big shock" he turned away from her.

"It was a big surprise to me too" She was still getting used to the idea, that she would be a Mammy in seven months.

"Jack, I know it's scary. I want you to be a part of our baby's life. If you need some time and space to think then take it."

"No" he blurted out straight away and Cara held her breath not sure what was coming next. He came to sit beside her on the bed, taking her hand in his. The simple gesture could mean anything and she feared he was about to gently let her down.

"I will go to the office and pick you up at six for dinner. We can talk again later" he leaned in kissing her forehead. His lips felt cold.

Cara followed him to the door and watched him climb into the back of his car. Lucas waved up at her, but Jack looked straight ahead as they drove away. Cara went back inside, feeling a distance between them.

Chapter Ten

In the blink of an eye his world was changing. He was going to be a Dad and it scared the shit out of him. How could he have let this happen? He thrummed his fingers against his desk, trying to calm himself down. He was angry with Cara, he knew it was irrational but he wasn't ready to be a Father yet. The woman was like a whirlwind, she came into his life so fast and changed everything, and he was still catching up. He looked up to a knock on his office door and watched as Dan walked in carrying a manila envelope.

Dan was a retired detective and looked the part. He wore a brown suit on his tall, slim body. His white hair and moustache completing the look.

"Jack" he reached across the desk, giving Jack a firm handshake.

"Dan" he smiled, putting thoughts of Cara and the baby to one side "what have you got for me?"

***

Cara looked at the clock again. Jack was gone over an hour and Cara sat biting her nails waiting for him to return. He said he would be back by six, which was an hour away and Cara was a nervous wreck. *What if he doesn't show?* She worried. She looked towards the door when the bell sounded, her heart banging hard in her chest. She walked on unsteady legs, hoping Jack had come back early. She yanked open the door and was surprised when Ann's red headed colleague, from a few weeks ago was standing there.

"Miss Stone" she smiled "Glad to have caught up with you."

"Hi" Cara paused for a moment trying to recall her name "I'm sorry I've forgotten your name" she apologised.

"That's okay, it's Nancy" she smiled sweetly.

"That's right I'm sorry, how can I help you?" she asked, confused about this lady's unannounced visit.

"I wondered if you have five minutes to answer some follow up questions on Mae's care?" she said, stepping over the threshold. Cara stood back a little, surprised by her eager advancement.

"Well actually Mae isn't here right now" she said blocking her entry.

"Oh, It's you I need to speak with…" she looked down at her red clipboard "…you are Mae's main care assistant now, correct?"

"Well yes" Cara couldn't explain it, but she felt uneasy. The woman seemed normal enough but there was something familiar about her. She wracked her brains to figure it out.

"Ok great, I won't take long and it would save me coming back again" she smiled. Cara brushed aside her paranoid suspicions. She seemed harmless enough and her hormones were playing havoc with her lately. She stepped aside and directed her into the kitchen.

Nancy was beautiful, her long red hair flowed down her back but her green eyes were her most striking feature.

Cara prepared two cups of coffee as they made idle chit chat about the holidays.

"Okay down to business" Nancy began as Cara sat across from her at the small round table, handing her a coffee.

"Do you plan to continue living with Mae and follow on as her main care provider?" Nancy read from her questionnaire.

"Well I'm not sure right now; I've had some personnel changes in my life. I would hope to remain a big part of Mae's care, but right now I'm not sure that's possible" Cara replied guiltily, Mae had always been there for her, she hoped to continue with Mae's care and have a healthy baby but she wasn't sure her pregnancy would allow the extra pressure.

"Okay, if there was to be a replacement carer, how soon would I need to put that place?" Nancy pursed her lips.

"Um, I'm not sure I would need to speak with Mae, I think we can manage for now, I'm pregnant but Mae is healthier than ever" Cara beamed realising life really was starting to look up.

"You're pregnant!!" Cara giggled at Nancy's shocked expression.

"Well its early days but yes" she smiled rubbing her pregnant belly.

Cara looked up from her tummy to a strange look in Nancy's eyes; she looked angry, livid even.

"Are you okay?" she asked her nervously.

"Yes" she forced a smile and Cara knew something wasn't right. Her skin began to crawl as her body rejected Nancy's presence. Cara sipped her coffee, looking over the rim at Nancy, who was still glaring at her.

"So do you like your job?" Cara asked changing the subject back to Nancy. The way she held herself seemed familiar somehow and yet she knew she had never spoken to this woman until a few weeks ago.

"Yes actually, I have my own personal experience with a certain cancer growing and taking over my world. I plan to have it removed permanently."

Cara couldn't miss the sinister tone in her voice. She looked towards the kitchen door behind Nancy with the sudden urge to bolt; she was alone with a complete stranger.

"Oh" Cara forced a sympathetic smile "I'm sorry to hear that."

"That's okay we all have our cross to bear… So are you and Jack together?" she asked sweetly.

"Well I wish you the best with the cancer" Cara ignored her question.

"It's not like Jack to settle" a twisted smile crossed Nancy's face, letting Cara know she had history with Jack.

"I think you should go" Cara stood reaching for the coffee mugs, before walking to the sink. The phone sounded on the kitchen wall and Cara reached for the receiver.

"Hello" her voice sounded shaky, even to her own ears.

"Cara, it's Jack, listen if a woman knocks, don't let her in, I'm on the way."

Cara heard the unmistakable sound of a knife being removed from the wooden block that sat on the counter top and turned "Jack" her voice was a whisper "help."
Nancy pulled the phone cord from the wall and Cara stepped back clutching the sink. Nancy was unrecognisable as she stood holding a large knife with a demonic look in her eyes.
"What are you doing?" Cara's voice trembled with fear, as she looked towards the door. Nancy was too close to her, to make clean getaway.
"Cutting the cancer out of my life" she hissed as she stepped closer.
"Look Jack will be home soon, please leave, we can forget this happened" Cara attempted to calm her and get her to leave. She began to laugh and Cara recognised the cackle. It was the woman Jack had brought home the week before.
"You think you can waltz into his life and push me out?" she started yelling and waving the knife close to Cara's face. The situation was becoming more volatile and Cara was frozen to the spot; her body felt like it weighed a ton. Her mind screamed at her to run but her legs stood rooted to the ground.
"I don't know what you mean."
"JACK" she roared "YOU THINK YOU CAN TRICK HIM WITH A BABY!"
"No, it's not like that" Cara sobbed as Nancy stepped closer holding the knife to her throat.
"The waterworks won't work with me" she spat.

"Why are you doing this?" Cara began to feel lighter, adrenaline coursed through her body, her eye's darting left to right trying to figure a way out.

"He was mine until you came along! You think I'm going to sit by while you take advantage of him?" she pressed harder against Cara's neck.

"I didn't, I swear you can have him" Cara cried.

"He's just a money machine to you, I tried to get him to see your true colours sooner but that failed" she growled angrily.

"It was you who stole the things" Cara's voice was a whisper, when she connected the dots. This woman must have been watching them, planning this all along.

"Yes you silly bitch and it worked! Until he went back sniffing for more" taunting Cara she lowered the knife against her stomach. This crazy woman went too far now, no one was going to threaten her baby. Cara grabbed the opportunity and pushed against Nancy with all her might and made a run for the kitchen door.

She took three steps before she felt the blade slice through her arm causing her to fall through the threshold and into the living room. She tried to get up straight away but was hampered, as Nancy grabbed her hair pulling her further into the room. Cara tried standing but Nancy tugged at her hair every time keeping her down, it felt as though it was being ripped from her skull.

"Please" she begged as her body slid along the wooden floors.

"Shut up" she screamed stopping to kick her in the stomach. Cara curled up in pain coughing and crying. She needed to protect her baby from this mad woman. "You are going to tell me how you fooled him, or I am going to cut that baby out of you."

***

Dan trailed through the security footage from Jack's building and was showing Jack stills of a woman, who used *his* key code to gain entry, when no one was home. He was the only person who knew that code and he was sickened when he recognised Jeri in the photos. In one photo Cara is arriving home just as Jeri was leaving and Jack rattled with anger knowing Cara had almost walked in on her.

"Where is she now?" Jack asked through clenched teeth.

"She moved into a new apartment in Queens about three weeks ago, she was still at home when I left to come here this afternoon" Dan answered as he gathered the photos back into his envelope.

"Where about in Queens?" Jack stood pushing his chair back.

"On Columbia Ave, why?" Dan noticed Jack's face pale.

"That's a block away from Cara" Jack was spurred into action as he ran for the door with Dan at his heels.

He needed to get to Cara and make sure she was ok; he called Lucas as he ran towards the elevators. Once inside the car he rang Mae's apartment.

"Hello" her voice broke through his racing mind, she sounded afraid.

"Cara, it's Jack, listen if a woman knocks, don't let her in, I'm on the way" he rushed.

"Jack... Help" Cara's whispered plea sent chills down his back as the line went dead. He re-dialled her number straight away and was met with an engaged tone.

"She is in trouble, ring the police..." he frantically directed Dan "...and have them sent to Cara's address."

"What's the delay?" he snapped at Lucas, frustrated to move faster. He tried Cara's mobile repeatedly but the line was ringing out. He felt helpless as he tried to get to Cara and his baby. He would never forgive himself if anything ever happened to either of them because of him.

"Hold on" Lucas said as he put his foot down and whizzed in and out of traffic.

"The police are on their way too" Dan snapped his phone shut and took his gun from his holster, checking it was loaded. Jack would kill anyone who tried to harm his family. They arrived at Mae's and both him and Dan leapt from the car, Lucas following not far behind.

***

Cara's shoulders shook as struggled to stand up. Her body felt weak and the sight blood, as it pooled on the wooden floor made her dizzy. Her vision blurred as she tried to focus on where Nancy was. Blood trickled down her arm and her stomach began to cramp from the blow it had received. She could hear her cell-phone ringing, she wanted to scream for help. She could see the pointed black heels of her attacker's shoes, as she pulled herself up against the sofa.

"I ought to slice that pretty face of yours and see if he falls for your charms then" her malevolent mumblings echoed throughout the house. Cara fought to stay awake, darkness called to her but she held on with all her might. "I will leave town, I promise, please help my baby" she cried, but her pleas were only met with more violence. Nancy grabbed her wound and squeezed, forcing Cara's eyes open wide. She screamed in agony as she tried to stand up, she needed to get away from here. She pushed weakly against Nancy who laughed at her meagre attempts to escape. Cara felt like a failure, she wanted to protect her baby and yet she couldn't get away from this raving lunatic. Her body was tugged back down again, her head banging hard against the floor as Nancy pulled at her blood soaked blonde locks. Cara could feel the cold steel of the knife against her throat as her vision blurred.

"Say goodbye to that pretty face of yours" Nancy cackled.

Jack burst through the door when he heard Cara's harrowing screams. Her bloodied face and body lay by the couch with a blood crazed Jeri hovering over her with a large knife. Without a second thought he dived forward and pulled Jeri backwards taking the knife away from Cara's throat at the same time.

Jeri punched and clawed at him as he tried to restrain her "LET ME GO" she wailed as Jack held her arms above her head. "I LOVE YOU JACK" she wriggled beneath him trying to free herself. Dan and Lucas came into the room behind him, both taking Jeri and holding her down. Jack kneeled beside Cara his heart stopping, as he took in all the blood. He quickly lifted her in his arms and laid her on the couch. He frantically searched her body and found the source of her blood loss. He left her for a moment to grab a small bath towel before securing it tightly with his tie.

"Cara" he called to her, patting her cheek "open your eyes baby" he pleaded. He could hear the police and ambulance sirens in the distance. Dan was speaking on the phone directing the police officers as he pinned, a still erratic, Jeri to the floor.

"I hope she is dead." she screamed as Jack continued to tend to Cara.

Ignoring Jeri he whispered in Cara's ear "I love you, please open your eyes" fears that he could lose her engrossed him. He watched her, stroking the hair from her face gently talking to her, letting her know he was here and he was rewarded when she moaned beneath him, her eyelashes fluttering open.

"Jack" she sobbed "the baby" and he gathered her in his arms loving her.

"It's okay baby, I'm here you both will be ok" he promised hiding his own anxieties about their child. It struck him how much he wanted this baby, how in a few short hours this baby was a part of his world and how he already wanted to protect his child from everything that threatened to harm it.

***

They arrived at the hospital and Jack stayed with Cara, he refused to leave her side until the Doctor ordered he go, so they could tend to her. Frustrated at being sent outside he paced the corridor, waiting on news. The doctors knew about the baby and Mae was en route to the hospital.

"Jack Cooper?" a female voice called, from behind him.

"Yes" he turned hoping to see a doctor, only to be met with two detectives.

"I'm detective Price, this is detective Claymore" she nodded to her male partner.

Jack gave them both a stiff nod, he was anxious for information on Cara but it was also important that the police investigated this fully.

"Have you charged that nut job yet?"

"Ms. Caldwell will be held for aggravated assault until we complete the investigation."

"She tried to murder my Girlfriend and unborn child." he snapped, he would not settle for anything less than attempted murder.

"We understand your frustration Mr. Cooper; right now we need to gather all the evidence before we officially charge her. We have looked into Jeri's previous convictions, are you aware that she has a restraining orders against her?"

"You mean she has done this before?" Jack turned and began pacing again; he was trying to contain his anger. He was no good to Cara if he got arrested, because right now he wanted to damage something or someone.

"Mr. Cooper we realise this is a trying time" Price spoke again from behind him "If we get as much information as possible we can hopefully make a stronger case for attempted murder."

"What do you need to know?"

"Ms. Caldwell was diagnosed with erotomaniac delusions after she had stalked a former boyfriend, simply put, she believed you loved her and I suspect she seen Cara as a threat. Did Cara have any suspicion that she could be in danger?"

Jack spent some time going over everything from the beginning, explaining about the break in's and Cara being framed. He gave them Dan's information to contact him for the CCTV footage and photos.

"What happens next?" he asked as they stood to leave.

"We will carry out a mental evaluation, under the circumstances and considering her previous offences, it is unlikely she will be released before prosecution."

The doctor came to retrieve him not long after the police left and Jack felt himself relax for the first time in hours. The baby was doing ok, Cara's wound had been stitched and she was stable. He sat at her bedside while she slept feeling like a fool, he had wasted so much time fighting his feelings for her. A life without Cara had flashed before his eyes when he seen her lying on the floor. He wouldn't let her go another day without knowing how much she meant to him, he would to tell her once and for all how he felt. She deserved better, their baby deserved better and he would make sure they got it.

***

The gentle pressure of Jack's hand in hers woke Cara from her slumber. The room was dark but she could see Jack as he leaned closer to check on her. He looked tired, his hair was a mess and his white shirt was crinkled and blood stained.

"Hey" she smiled, licking her dry lips.

"Hey" he whispered back, kissing her head, her cheeks and lips "how do you feel? are you okay?"

Cara nodded "is the baby okay?" her eyes watered terrified to hear bad news.

"So far, everything looks okay, you need to rest and try to relax."

"Jack I was so afraid."

"The police have her now, you don't ever have to worry about her again."

"I never saw it coming she was like a mad woman" tears flowed freely from her eyes now as she relived the horror of that day's events in her mind. It was hard to believe that she had almost died at the hands of someone she'd never even known.

Jack wiped her tears and leaned forward kissing her gently "I'm so sorry Cara, please forgive me" he begged.

"It's not your fault" she sniffed.

"I should never have left you, I should have stayed and talked about the baby, I should have sensed something was wrong with her and I never should have doubted you."

"It hurt to think you thought that way, but I knew after Christmas Day that you believed me Jack."

Cara brought his hand to her face kissing it softly "It's ok Jack" she could see the guilt begin to eat at him.

"Cara I'm not going anywhere ever again, you're stuck with me forever."

"Good because we need you."

"I need you both too, I love you Cara."

It felt like the most natural thing in the world to tell Cara he loved her. Why he ever thought it would be hard to say, amazed him now. He was an intelligent man, but sometimes even he needed to admit when he was wrong. Today he learned an important lesson in his life, his new family, were all that mattered.. He would cherish and protect them and never let either of them down again.

***

Cara sat talking with Mae for hours every day during her stay in hospital. She was having nightmares about what had happened and Mae was helping to alleviate some of her fears. Jack was arranging her to see a therapist when they went home, but for now she was happy to share her worries with Mae.

There was a long road to feeling secure ahead but with Jack and the people she loved at her side she knew she would be ok. She hated to see Mae so concerned and begged her not to stay all day but she refused to be at home. Jack had moved Mae into his condo, insisting she shouldn't be in the apartment alone, which helped put Cara's mind at ease. Jack loved her and she wanted to go home and begin to rebuild her life with him. He tormented the nurses about how the baby was doing and although they hadn't made any official plans yet, he loved them both and she knew they would figure it out eventually. His actions over the past few days had been enough, to show her how much he cares.

"Okay Ms. Stone looks like we can let you go home today" the doctor declared happily as he entered her room.

"Great" she and Mae said in unison. She looked to Jack, who was quietly assessing the doctor.

"What time can we sign her out?" Mae chirped.

"Is she really ready to go home, what about the baby?" Jack stood from the bed his hand still in Cara's.

"Yes she will need to stay off her feet, get plenty of rest and return once a week for a scan to check the baby."

"If you're certain" Jack smiled now from ear to ear "I'll make sure she follows all your instructions" he turned back to Cara.

"I will have the nurse take care of all the paperwork, so you should be good to go in about one hour" the doctor smiled, shaking everyone's hand before leaving.

Jack lifted Cara into the backseat as Lucas held open the door to the black Mercedes.

"So happy to see you looking healthy again Ms. Stone" Lucas smiled.

"Thanks Lucas and it's Cara" she narrowed her eyes playfully, she hated how formal her name sounded.

Jack sat in the back with her and Mae sat up front with Lucas "where are we going?" she asked, realising she didn't want to return to her home.

"We will stay in the city tonight at mine and then tomorrow we will go to Hudson Valley" Jack declared.

"But how will you get to work?"

"David has everything in hand for the next week and then I will commute until we get somewhere closer that's big enough for all of us."

Jack placed his hand over her stomach and Cara leaned forward kissing him hard. She loved that he accepted Mae as part of their family.

"I love you" she mouthed against his lips and he returned the gesture.

***

Jack carried Cara straight to his bed, Mae had gone on with Lucas to visit with Vanessa giving them some alone time. They lay holding each other "I was so worried" Jack confessed rubbing his nose against hers. Cara lifted her mouth to his and he took her offered lips. It felt so good to have him just kiss and cuddle her, neither wanting to break the contact. She could feel his unmet desire against her thigh and was tempted to push for more, to meet both their needs fully.
"Jack" she croaked looking up into his lust filled eyes.
"No" he said, immediately reading her body as it pressed into his, her eyes calling for him to connect them completely. She pouted at his serious expression and knew he would deny them both, until he was certain she was fully recovered.
"You never told me how you feel about the baby?"
Jack had told her he would be here for them both and that he loved her but Cara wanted to know, if he was ok with being a Father.
He sat up and leaned over her as she lay beneath him, his fingers lifting her night shirt exposing her tummy. His eyes held hers before he smiled kissing her lips as his fingers caressed her tiny bump.

"I was shocked but now I know this is what I want, more than anything" he said as his lips moved to her tummy kissing their growing baby. The gesture brought tears of happiness to Cara's eyes as he feathered light kisses, all over her stomach. She remained still, ecstatic as he lauded attention on their baby.

"I wonder if it's a little girl or a boy?" he smiled up at her looking genuinely amazed and excited.

"If it's a boy I bet he will look like you" she smiled back, imagining a mini Jack running around.

"Or a little blonde singing angel, either way they will be blessed with good looks" he laughed covering her tummy again and gathering her back into his arms.

"Or twins" she teased, laughing as a look of dread settled on Jack's face.

"Don't jinx us, one baby at a time."

"Ok, I was thinking we could have six and start straight away after this baby is born" she smiled lovingly into his eyes, pretending not to notice him pale. She burst out laughing at his shocked silence and he realised she was winding him up.

"Ha ha very funny, mocking is catching! But I won't mind making the six babies" he nibbled her ear and she groaned as he teased her back, torturing her as the burn intensified within her. He pulled back with a mischievous grin "behave" he warned her pulling her back against his chest.

They snuggled for the rest of the night making plans for their future and arguing about baby names.

The End

Epilogue

The heat from the sun, as it belts down from the blue August sky, scorches my exposed skin. I veer off the cycle track and rest my beautiful yellow bike in the grass. Jack has cycled ahead with baby Matthew harnessed to his chest. I feel like the happiest woman in the world today, my hunky boyfriend has turned into world's greatest Dad and still manages to shower me with just as much love and attention, if not more.

The sun continues to heat my warm skin as I move under the shade of a nearby tree, I need to rest for a moment. Jack is much fitter than me; it will probably take me an hour to find him. Central park is packed today and I watch as families enjoy the summer sun.

My tummy rumbles and I remember the delicious picnic Jack has prepared for us. He was acting a little strange all morning, insisting I sit back while he took care of everything. He usually hates simple responsibilities, like which meat to put on a sandwich. Thinking of food again causes my stomach to growl, louder this time and I collect my bike and go in search of my family.

I see Jack sitting beside a lake as I cross a small stone bridge. He waves to me and I make my way to him. He looks sexy in his white t-shirt and blue chinos, and I feel hungry for him now.

"Hey" he kisses me as I remove my helmet.

"Hey, I'm starved" I kiss him back before moving to the blanket, kissing Matthews pudgy face. His blue eyes stare up at me from his bouncer and I play with him while Jack prepares lunch.

"I think he needs a nappy change" Jack say's from behind me and I roll my eyes.

"Waiting on me to arrive, were you?" I turn, narrowing my eyes at him.

He begins to laugh with a guilty look on his face and I know I'm right. I don't mind, but I won't admit that to Jack or I'll be receiving this kind of gift on a daily basis. Matthew coos up at me as I unbutton his little blue onesie. My child is too adorable; I unbutton his vest and my heart stops for a second as my eyes catch the message on it;

"Will you marry my Daddy?"

I lean back on my heels and turn to face Jack. He is kneeling behind me, one leg raised and his hand reaching towards me holding a small, open, black box. A beautiful diamond winks at me and I look up into Jack's eyes;

"Will you marry me?" he says.

His white smile is broad and I begin to cry "yes, yes, yes" as I jump up, knocking him over as I wrap my arms around his neck. He rolls me over, kissing me.

"Let's get this on you so" he smiles as we sit up. Taking my hand he slides the beautiful antique cut diamond down my finger. I admire it as he lifts Matthew into his arms. I couldn't be happier.

"Cara Cooper, sounds kinda sexy" he winks at me.

Except from Christine's next book available for download May 12th 2015:

Desperately Undone

"I know that I'm in a city. I can hear police and ambulance sirens all day long. My head hurts so bad, I open my eyes and I'm in a dark room. There is a small ray of light, peeping through a hole, in the dark curtains hanging in front of me. I have no idea what time it is but the sun is shining. I want to rub my eyes but my hands are tied behind my back. Oh God, my head hurts so much. The smell turns my stomach and I realise I've wet myself. I can see a small cot in the corner, but I don't want to lie down there, it looks dirty, I just want to go home."

I open my eyes and my therapist Sue is smiling at me. I feel safe again in her room. Light floods through the wide open curtains and everything in here is white. The walls, the couch, even Sue is wearing a white summer dress. The only splash of colour is the green plants she has placed throughout the room. I sit up, straightening my pale blue blouse. This is the first therapist, that I have ever truly felt connected to and I'm grateful for her.

She is so laid back, she always dresses casually and she never pushes me.

"Well done, that was some great progress" she congratulates. I don't feel like it was great progress, I should have unlocked more information by now.

"Sue, I don't understand why my memory won't return" I pout like a child. I'm sure Sue is tired of explaining to me why my mind chooses to keep hidden, the secrets I so desperately want to unravel.

"Aubrey, you went through an emotional and physical trauma. It was an overwhelmingly stressful event and your brain is protecting you from it."

I've heard all this before, I know she is right but I'm so ready now to face my past and move on.

"I just want to remember so bad, June 5th is two weeks away and I don't want to be out there..." I stand and move to the window looking out at the Boston sky line "...not knowing everything that happened in that room."

Sue remains in her seat, her lips are pursed as she taps her fingers on her white clipboard.

"Have you gone back to the room Aubrey?"

I wasn't expecting her to ask me this and I'm surprised. I've thought about it a lot over the last ten years but I've never had the guts to go there.

"No" I shrug simply and return to the couch.

"Part of your therapy is to face the unbearable memories that your mind is avoiding, maybe going there will help unlock some of the answers."

Instantly I feel my body tense and heat creep up my neck. The fear is there again, and although I chase my past, these feelings remind me, it's not ready for me to catch up.

"Sue, how will I ever move on if I can't even go to a stupid room?" a frustrated tear rolls down my face as I clench my blouse in a knot.

"You need to stop being so hard on yourself, you will move past this, there is no quick fix for PTSD but there is an end in sight we just have to take it one session at a time."

I consider whether I should tell her about my dream again, my time is almost up and I don't like running over.

"Out with it"

I look up at her and her eyebrows are raised as she sits waiting for me to spill my guts.

"I had a dream about him again last night" I blush. I always feel so ashamed and messed up when I talk about him. The dreams are always so vivid, and they are always in that room.

"Was it the same as last time?".

"No" I shake my head, considering how much of my fucked up dreams I want to share.

"He was sitting at the end of the cot, just looking at me. I am, as always, afraid but when he is in the room I feel safer". I throw my head into my hands to hide my face from her, I can't even imagine what she must think.

"These dreams might be memories Aubrey, but they could also be your mind's way of working through some of your experiences subconsciously."

I have seen news reports, court documents, pictures, everything related to my case. I have leafed through them all, grappling for any small piece of information that might help me.

"He helped me" I whisper, because I know it sounds ridiculous.

"Yes, he did but he also helped himself Aubrey. He received a more lenient sentence for his testimony. What he did was wrong, he's a criminal, you don't have to feel guilty for his actions."

I don't feel guilty, he deserved what he got; but in my dreams I like when he is with me, in my dreams we have a bond and I need to know what else happened in that room, before June 5th.

About The Author

Christine Winston is an Irish romantic novels author. She lives in Finglas, Dublin with her daughter Isabelle.

Follow Christine on Facebook, Twitter and Instagram for news on all of her upcoming books.

www.facebook.com/christinewinstonauthor

www.twitter.com/christinewinst5

www.instagram.com/christine_winston

Thank You for reading.

Made in the USA
Charleston, SC
14 August 2015